SCHOOL FOR RELUCTANT WITCHES

MISTY'S MAGICK & MAYHEM: BOOK 1

Carolina Mac & Auburn Tempest

ISBN 978-1-989187-17-3

To: Solitary Witches Everywhere

*Blessed are the Witches, for they are the keepers of
the Old Ways of Love for the Earth and all her creatures.*

—www.witchcraft-wicca.com

CHAPTER ONE

Saturday, December 31st.

New Year's Eve.

<u>Nine Saint Gillian Street, New Orleans</u>

Misty cleansed the energy on her father's ceremonial athame and dried the bolline, ready for the following day. She laid them both on the black satin altar cloth on the sideboard under the window and stared out at her back yard. The moon was high, its silver glow draining the color from her large lawn, herb garden, and the laneway beyond.

She loved this time of night. When the world slowed, and she had time to admire the gifts in her life.

The witching hour, as it were.

With her tools taken care of, she washed and dried the supper dishes and pots and put them away. She adored her newly renovated kitchen with the granite counters, the six-burner stove, and the dark red walls.

The perfect workplace.

When she'd modernized the kitchen, she couldn't

bear to part with her father's old wooden worktable. Ten feet long, and almost two-hundred years old, each scratch and scar marked years of use. Instead of exchanging it for something new, it remained the centerpiece of the room, and she used it daily to make potions, salves, and remedies.

The battered old surface reminded her of her childhood growing up in this massive Victorian home. She'd sit and color a picture while her father prepared ingredients for his next spell or potion. He'd recite the ingredients, the procedure, the phase of the moon, and the ritual. It was amazing how much she'd retained, purely by osmosis.

The sweet-scented fragrance of the dried flowers and herbs she'd collected during Mabon drifted down from the ceiling. The bunches hung in neatly organized rows, ready for the taking when she needed an ingredient.

"Why are you moping, Mystere?"

"I'm not moping, Daddy."

"Are you sure . . . about ending it with Blaine?"

She nodded. "I love him, but I don't belong in Texas. I belong here in this house with you. I belong to New Orleans and the bayou and my heritage. People know me here. They look up to me and depend on me."

"All true, my darling. The magick community reveres you, but you need to have a life too. Go out and meet new people. Have some fun. It's New Year's Eve."

She finished with the dish towel and tucked it over

the handle of her stove. "It's not the new year for us. We celebrated at Samhain."

"Contrariness doesn't become you, Mystere. New Orleans is celebrating. Go out. People will be reveling in the streets."

Misty glanced into her father's favorite corner, and his presence was reassuring, regardless of him being a ghost. His silvery-green image shimmered in the light, there yet not solid. "How do you know what day it is, Daddy?"

"Oh, come on, Mystere. I may be bodily dead, but I'm not brain dead." He laughed at his joke, and Misty laughed too. "Now, go on, child. Get yourself upstairs and put on something pretty. You wear too much black."

She glanced down at herself and shrugged. "These are my work clothes. Customers expect a certain image when they come for readings."

"You aren't charging enough for the readings."

"What makes you say that?"

"I worry. If you value your time and talents, others will too. I don't want you struggling."

"You left me well provided for, Daddy. Besides, I haven't touched the insurance money from Brad. Stop worrying." She didn't want to think about her dead-beat ex-husband.

Especially not on a night of beginnings.

"I'm glad that wastrel is dead. He was a thorn in my side since the day you met him."

Misty chuckled. "I should've kept track of how

many times you said you hated him, Daddy. In the end, you were right. He was a terrible person and wrong for me."

"That's it right there, Mystere."

"What is?"

"You need to go out and find the *right* person for you. The perfect match. Your soulmate. Someone with powers to enhance your own. What a dynamic coupling that would make. I'm excited just thinking about it."

"Always the romantic, aren't you, Daddy? And where will I meet Mr. Perfect? Any suggestions?"

"It won't be in this kitchen. Go downtown. The streets will be teeming with revelers tonight, and you'll find him."

"Will you help me find him?"

"Of course, wand out, and repeat after me."

> *Broken heart, fresh start,*
> *Give true love a little shove,*
> *The perfect match is mine to catch,*
> *Draw him near, the course is clear,*
> *So mote it be.*

Misty finished her father's spell and smiled. "Thank you, Daddy. That was lovely."

"That will draw your heart's match like a wasp buzzing towards a can of Coke."

Misty giggled. "Well, I better go up and get ready."

Frenchmen Street

The street was alive with New Orleans locals and tourists alike. Celebrating the night away, the crowds pulsed and swayed to upbeat Dixieland jazz played by five men on the balcony of one of the clubs. Misty stepped out of the cab at her favorite wine bar and handed the driver his fare. She owned a car, a blue Honda, but hated driving. Traffic made her nervous, especially on a night like tonight. She didn't need the stress. She didn't need anything beyond wine and cheese and live music.

Misty jostled through the dozens of people waiting in the entrance to make it to the reception stand. She didn't see any empty tables. Of course, because there were so many people bustling about, she couldn't see much of anything at all.

When she was about to turn away, the manager called to her, "Madam LeJeune, I have a table for you."

Misty smiled and squeezed past several people waiting in line. "Thank you for saving me, Jason."

"My pleasure, Madam. Your presence here is sure to bring good fortune for the New Year."

Misty patted his arm. "I'll put in a good word for you with Dionysus."

A female server hustled over to her table to take her order, then hurried away. Misty eyed the men passing by her table with renewed interest. Any of them could be a wasp about to fly directly to her can of Coke.

"I should've ordered Coke instead of wine," she said to herself before giggling with a wave of apprehension.

The band finished the second set of the evening and set their instruments down to take a short break. When the house music came on, Misty scanned the people standing in groups laughing and talking with wine glasses in their hands.

"Is this seat taken?"

Misty looked up into a pair of deep brown eyes.

Is he the one?

"Not yet," she drawled.

"Mind if I borrow the chair?"

She frowned and waved off his grip. "Oh, yes, I do. I'm expecting someone."

He kept his hold on the back of the chair, ready to drag it away. "They'd be here by now if they were coming, wouldn't they? It's almost midnight."

"He's a vampire and doesn't come out until twelve."

He gave her a droll stare. "Come on, lady. Don't screw with me. Let me have the fucking chair."

Misty noticed the server close behind the chair-grabber. The girl was juggling a whole tray of full champagne glasses. Misty concentrated on the tray and whoops—it tipped.

The server squealed as she dumped all the bubbly onto the chair thief.

Champagne splashed, glasses smashed, and the man bothering her hollered curses at the top of his lungs. With his mind on other things, he relinquished the chair and tore to the men's room, brushing at his soaked suit jacket.

Giggling, Misty picked up her wine glass and took a sip.

"That was nice work, Miss LeJeune." A handsome man with shoulder-length dark hair sat down opposite her. He waved to the server and ordered a Guinness. "Fabian Landry, at your service. Would you care for another glass of wine?"

"Do I know you, Mr. Landry?"

He flashed a winning smile. "I know you. Well, everyone in the magick community knows you or wants to know you. Your family is legendary."

"And did you come here to find me, tonight?" she asked, wondering if he was the one her father's spell had given a little shove or just someone tracking her down.

"I almost spoke with you one other time. I saw you here once before with a young Latino man. He appeared rather formidable, so I didn't risk talking to you then."

"Wise decision," said Misty. Talking about Blaine on New Year's when she was out looking for a new man hurt. But relationships changed, and they were no longer together—except for in spirit. He lived in Austin, and though she tried to build a life there for a while, she needed to be home.

"I'm sorry. Have I upset you?"

"Not at all," she said, pulling herself out of her moping, as her father said. "And you can call me Misty if you wish."

He smiled, and she caught a spark of something in his right eye. A reflection perhaps.

The server brought a coaster and Fabian's tall glass of dark beer while the band retook the stage and began revving everyone up for the New Year's countdown.

"Almost time," said Fabian. He motioned to the server to refill her glass. "You'll need a full glass to toast the new year. What will you wish for?"

"That the new year is better than the last."

"Only time will tell." Fabian, set his glass down and offered her his hand. "Shall we dance?"

I love to dance. Is he the one?

Deciding not to analyze things, she accepted. Movement was severely restricted on the crowded patch of hardwood the bar called a dancefloor. Fabian held Misty close, and she inhaled the essence of the man. His skin tingled slightly of earth magick—but only slightly—and something she couldn't put her finger on.

Fabian's cologne was pleasant but didn't smell nearly as expensive and seductive as Blaine's. He didn't possess Blaine's physical power or presence, but something brewed beneath the surface of the man that she found alluring, if not a little frightening.

At the stroke of midnight, cheap noisemakers rang out in a cacophony, and everyone cheered in the new year.

Fabian kissed her lightly on the mouth. "Happy New Year, Misty LeJeune."

"And to you, Fabian Landry. Shall we take a walk?"

"I would love to."

They walked down the street together, enjoying the

cool evening air and the energy rising from the celebrating crowd. "I love the city," said Fabian. "I feed off its perpetual energy."

Misty breathed deep and knew what he meant. "It's where I belong."

After they'd taken a trip around the block, they ended up back at the corner by the bar. Fabian stopped and gestured to the line of cars parked along the road. "Did you drive?"

"I came by cab."

"At this time of night on New Year's Eve, it will take you some time to find another. May I drive you?"

"That's generous of you."

Fabian shrugged. "Honestly, it's selfish. I want you safe, plus, you want this year to start on the right foot."

Well, when he put it that way.

"Yes. Thank you. That would be nice."

"Perfect," he said, pointing to a red sports car down the row. "Tell me, where are we headed?"

When they arrived at Saint Gillian Street, Fabian parked in front of number nine and turned off the car. "This was a nice night. Can I see you again?"

"We'll have to see if it's in the cards. Thank you for seeing me home."

"I'll walk you to the door."

"No need. My dog is inside and will protect me," she unbuckled her seatbelt and got out. "Namaste."

Fabian slid out and rounded the front of the car.

"But, your dog's not out here, and it's a long way up the dark pathway."

Misty didn't know whether to be flattered or annoyed at his persistence. "It's late, there's no one on the street, and I can protect myself."

"All the same, I'd feel better."

Misty refused to relent. When he moved to escort her, she pressed a hand against his chest and locked his feet to the ground. Stuck in place, his eyes bugged wide. With her independence firmly established, she leaned in and kissed him gently on the cheek. "Thank you for a nice evening, Fabian."

Fabian chuckled. "I'll call you tomorrow."

CHAPTER TWO

Sunday, January 1st.
New Year's Day.

<u>Nine Saint Gillian Street</u>

Misty rose with the roosters and buzzed around the kitchen, making tea and a list of resolutions. A new year and with it, a new life was beginning. The crackling energy around her signified the potential building. Choices to be made. Paths to be taken. Life held offerings for her, and they were powerful. Big things were about to happen. She could feel it.

"Did you meet him?" Her father appeared in his favorite corner as she poured boiling water into the big black teapot her mother had always used.

"I did meet someone downtown, Daddy. He might not be my soulmate, but we had a nice evening."

"Invite him to the house. I want to watch him and listen to what he says to you. You're far too trusting of men and could use a second opinion."

"Second opinion of nothing. I met a man, we had a

drink together, and then he drove me home. It's as simple as that."

"But is he a *good* man? There will be no more charlatans like Brad in your life, Mystere. I will make sure of it."

Misty bustled about, wiping the counter down while she waited for the tea to steep. "And how will you stop it from happening, Daddy?"

His sly smile was as endearing in death as it had been when he'd been alive. "My powers are diminished, but not gone, my darling daughter. I will watch this new man of yours with a wary eye and see if he measures up under my attention."

"Thank you, Daddy. What would I do without you?"

"When are you to see him next?"

"He said he'd call me today."

"Then you better think on what you're offering him for evening meal. Call him, Misty. Invite him to dinner."

Misty giggled. "I'll think about that, but first I have to call Blaine and make amends. It's one of my resolutions."

"I don't make those anymore."

"That's one advantage you have, Daddy. Ghosts don't have to bother with self-improvement."

Blaine answered on the second ring and sounded sleepy. "Oh, I'm sorry, Beb. I forgot about the hour. Did I wake you?"

"It's okay. What can I do for you, Misty?"

Misty drew a breath and crossed Blaine off her to-do list. "I called to apologize. I put you through such heartache with Kim, and I regret it. I release you from your promise. I should have helped Annie with no strings attached because she was always so good to me. I'm sorry I let my hurt feelings get so out of hand."

"I appreciate that. Thank you. That's generous of you and a huge relief."

As she heard Blaine say the words, she felt the weight of her behavior lessen and shared his relief. She would make things right with him. A new year and a new beginning.

"And Blaine?"

"Yeah?"

"If you need me to help with anything, I'm here. Just call and tell me what's needed."

"That's a load off my mind. I've come to depend on you when I've got no clues to work with. I appreciate the offer."

"Happy New Year, Beb."

"Same, Misty, and thanks for calling."

With tears in her eyes, Misty crossed the kitchen and poured herself a mug of boiling hot tea. She loved Blaine but knew she didn't belong in Austin. This was her home.

Number nine Saint Gillian Street.

Jambalaya simmered and bubbled on the stove as Misty made her mother's favorite bread pudding recipe. If she decided to follow her father's advice and invite Fabian Landry to dinner, he'd find out that she was one helluva good cook.

Hoodoo barked like a wild dog and ran into the foyer. "Who's here, boy?" She peeked through the old lace curtain covering the sidelight. Eww, she made a face. She needed to replace most of the curtains in the house. These were all dusty, musty, and worn.

Another thing for her New Year's list.

"You need new curtains on your windows, don't you old house?" She waited for the familiar creaking as the house answered her.

Misty smiled as she saw the large Cajun woman and her son coming up the front steps. Angelique was a wonder of magick in her own right. She was also the best assistant and friend any witch ever had. When they reached the porch, she opened the door and opened her arms.

"Angelique, *ma chere*, come in. Welcome home."

"Marc fetch me from my sister's and bring me back," Angelique said in her Cajun dialect. Not many understood her. Her two sons, Luc and Marc, and Misty were three of the few.

Misty stepped aside as Angelique entered. When her bayou treasure passed, she nodded to her son. "Hello, Marc. It's so nice to see you. Come in. I have tea ready in the pot."

"Madam." Marc nodded, and set his mother's bag down at the foot of the stairs. He followed them into the kitchen, a burlap sack in his hand. *"Maman* and I gathered roots you be needin, Madam LeJeune."

"Ooh, thank you so much." Misty peered into the sack and breathed deep. "Some rare ones indeed. And Bloodroot, I'm so in need of that one. I'm indebted to you both."

Marc shook his head. *"Non."*

Misty poured tea and opened a container of cookies she'd baked a couple of days before. She gestured to them to take what they wished. "How is your sister now, *Chere?*"

"Much better, *merci.*"

Misty's phone rang, and she excused herself. She got the name and jotted down a time. "Customer coming in an hour."

"I prepare the front parlor, Madam." Angelique finished her tea and took her cup to the sink. "New Year is busy time. People wantin to know about the year comin. You been busy?"

Misty checked on the jambalaya and stirred the contents in the pot. "Not yet." The phone rang again, and it was another customer wishing a reading on the first day of the new year. "Well, maybe the rush is just beginning."

Angelique smiled. "I return just in time, Madam."

After a short visit to ensure his mother had settled in, Marc took his leave and headed back to Texas. He'd been gone only minutes when the first of Misty's New

Year customers arrived.

Vivian LaFrance was in her sixties and had been a steady customer for a number of years. As a nervous widow, she found comfort in discussing matters involving her deceased husband—Fred. She was a loyal customer, and while Misty lived in Austin, Vivian called several times a week for readings over the phone.

The gist of today's visit stemmed from the overtures of interest several men at the senior's center had made toward Vivian and whether or not she should risk Fred's jealousy and start seeing someone? If so, which one should she pick?"

"Sit down, Vivian," said Misty, gesturing to the sunny spot at the table. "If you like, Angelique could bring you some peppermint tea to help you relax."

"Thank you, dear." Vivian nodded and offered Angelique a friendly smile. "It's not easy, you know, getting past the trauma of life. Fred and I had plans. I come from a generation where married couples stay married. If you love a man, then you love him, and that's that. Even a single thought of moving on with another fills me with guilt."

Misty shuffled her tarot deck as Vivian said her piece.

"I think that's perfectly natural," she said, glancing over to her Daddy in the corner. "Just because someone dies doesn't mean they don't still hold a tangible place in your heart. So, what is your question for me today?"

"I want to know what Fred wants. He was always the decision-maker. He was smart, and I trust his judgment."

Misty focused on Vivian's question, and when the cards settled in her palms, she set them on the velvet runner in front of Vivian. Running a gentle finger over the deck, she fanned them out.

"With your question in mind, choose a card and place it here." She pointed to a point on the ebony altar cloth between them. "And another here." They repeated this until the spread was complete and laid out in a cross formation.

Turning them over, one at a time, she studied them. "Look at that, Vivian, in the position of present you chose the Lovers card. This signifies relationships and choice and illustrates the power of love, romance, and attraction."

"But what does that mean? Which relationship? Which choice? What does Fred want me to do?"

"I believe Fred wants you to move on and find happiness."

Vivian stared at the card as if it were going to pop to life and give her all the answers.

Tarot didn't work like that.

"See here. This is your past card. Four of Cups. This card signifies boredom and feeling dissatisfied with your life." Misty pointed at the mermaid depicted in the card. "See the pearls in her hair, they represent dreams of what yet might be, but there's no action."

"Like I'm stuck in a rut?"

"Yes. Is that how you feel?"

"I suppose so. I've gotten used to being alone, you know?"

Misty nodded. "And here, in your future, you chose the Six of Swords."

"Is that good?"

Misty smiled. "There's no good or bad in Tarot, Vivian. I've told you that before. There is intention and interpretation."

"What does the six mean?"

"The Six of Sword signifies movement and progress. It's a journey, either internal or external."

"Could it mean a cruise?"

Misty nodded. "Yes, it could. You see here. The character is gliding his boat over water. It can imply smooth sailing ahead or perhaps, as you mentioned, a cruise."

"One of those men I told you about—Gregory—he wants to take me on a seniors' cruise out of Miami."

Misty smiled. "Well, that sounds like a lot of fun. Do you want to go?"

"I'm thinking I might. You really think Fred wants me to move on?"

Misty drew her hand over the reading. "That's the way I'm interpreting it for you because that was your question. Should you move on? The answer is *yes*. Let Fred become a part of your past and begin a new chapter in your life."

Vivian picked up her tea and sipped it. "I'm so glad I came today. What else do you see ahead of me this year?"

Misty finished the reading, and Vivian sat back, happy with the results. She paid for the appointment, and Misty saw her out to her car. As the beige sedan pulled away from the curb and disappeared down the street, a red sports car drove up.

Fabian. He said he was going to call.

Too late to worry about that now. He jumped out of his car, looking handsome and full of energy. He waved as he locked up and ran up the walk with a wrapped package in his hand. "I know I said I'd call, but I couldn't wait to see you again. I brought you a present."

Misty didn't like the energy she was getting off him at all this morning. "I don't need a gift. It's inappropriate. We barely know each other."

He waved away her objections and followed her up the walk and straight into the foyer. "Nonsense, if the Fates smile on us, we might get to know each other better, very soon."

Angelique straightened from where she was tidying up the front parlor and getting ready for the next customer.

"Angelique," Misty said, gesturing to her friend. "This is Fabian Landry, the man I met last night while I was out."

They shook hands, and, at his touch, Angelique stiffened with a strange expression Misty hadn't seen before.

When neither of them said anything, she thought

maybe she imagined it. "Please, Fabian, come into the kitchen. I have tea made if you like?"

"I'm a coffee man, myself."

Misty nodded. "I can do that too. I've had a busy morning, and I have another client arriving in a few minutes."

Fabian sat down at the table and pushed the wrapped gift towards her. "Open it, please."

Misty claimed the seat opposite him and tore the blue paper off the gift box. She removed the wand from the box and held it gently in her hand. "Oh, it's lovely. The crystals are beautiful, and I can feel the energy."

"Let me see you do something," said Fabian. "I know your magick is powerful."

Misty laughed and headed over to the counter. "I don't do parlor tricks on command. The best I can do for you is to make a mug of coffee appear before you. That will have to do."

"I don't do parlor tricks either," said Fabian with a little edge to his voice. "I have helped the police with several cases in the past, and I'm slowly building a reputation here in New Orleans. I have magick too."

Misty pressed the button on the coffee maker, wondering how he seemed so much more appealing last night.

It must have been the wine.

"What kind of cases have you worked on?" she asked.

"Mostly missing persons and some kidnapped

children."

She couldn't fault that. In fact, she found it gratifying to lend her gifts when law enforcement needed a little mystic help. "The police must have been grateful."

"They were."

"What else do you do?"

Misty's big, sucky, Bernese Mountain Dog trotted into the kitchen. The fur on the ruff of his neck stood on end as he inched towards Fabian.

"What's wrong with your dog?" Fabian asked, looking baffled. "Dogs love me. Do you have a biscuit I can give him?"

Right, my boy. I get it.

"I'm sorry, he doesn't usually growl. Angelique, would you put Hoo in the yard, dear?"

"Certainly, Madam."

Misty poured a mug of coffee for Fabian and set it on the table with cream and sugar. "I'm afraid I don't have much time to visit before my next client arrives."

Fabian sipped at the edge of the mug and nodded. "Of course. This is a lovely old house."

"It's been in my family for generations. This house holds a lot of memories."

"Memories, yes," he said, pinning her with that smile of his. "The famous LeJeune witches and their Book of Shadows. I bet that priceless tome is hiding somewhere under this roof, right? You're so fortunate to have generations of knowledge at your fingertips."

The hair on the back of Misty's neck stood on end.

"Every magickal family has a book. As you know, it's a private treasure to be shared and passed down to their own. And yes, that's special."

"I'd be honored if you showed it to me some time. Not now, of course, but after we get to know each other better and you realize you can trust me."

Misty checked her watch and started clearing the table. "I'm sorry, but I must get ready for the next reading. It's a busy time of year for me. When my schedule clears up, and I have free time, I'll give you a call."

As soon as he'd swallowed the last sip of his coffee, Misty showed Fabian out. Angelique joined her at the front door and shook her head. Together they watched him walk down the flagstone path to his shiny red car.

"D'at man has deceit in his aura, Madam. No trust him."

Misty wrapped an arm across her shoulders. "I got that too. Do you think his magick is stronger than it feels?"

Angelique shook her head of long black hair. "No, but de threat he pose to you, and de house is."

Misty let in Hoodoo, assured him that the bad man was gone. Her father's silvery-green shimmer had returned to the corner of the kitchen. "Were you listening, Daddy?"

"And I heard what you already know. His intentions are suspect, my beautiful one. Do not trust him."

"I won't." Misty held up the wand. "But he brought me a present. What do you think of this?"

"You have my wand, child. You need no other."

Misty headed into the front parlor with the new wand in her hand and caught Angelique about to light the candles for the pending customer. "Wait a moment, *Chere*. Let me try out this wand."

She held it out in front of her and focused her energy.

Candles wax with smoke and fire
Ignite I beg you, and Flame burn higher

With a *poof*, all the candles in the room ignited at once.

Angelique smiled. "Wonderful. So much positive energy."

The doorbell rang, and the next customer arrived. Misty invited the well-dressed gentleman inside. "Lovely to see you, Leo. Did you enjoy your holidays?"

Leo Pinoit was a handsome man in his fifties, wealthy and retired, he played golf almost every day and wrote a column for one of the gourmet magazines in the city.

"Not as much as I would have if you'd been with me, Madam LeJeune."

"You're a flirt. Did you play golf today?"

"Unfortunately, no. The courses were closed for the most part. They think nothing of inconveniencing their patrons."

"Maybe they needed a family day."

"Speaking of a family day, when will you let me take you to dinner on one of my restaurant test runs?"

Misty chuckled. "Soon. I would love to go when you try the menu at a new place."

Leo cast an admiring eye at Angelique. "And of course, Madam Angelique would be welcome too."

"Merci, Monsieur Pinoit," said Angelique.

Misty sat down at the table and shuffled the cards.

"I'll get de tea," Angelique said. "Peppermint, *Monsieur?*"

"Peppermint is fine, Madam. I bend to your will."

Angelique giggled as she edged towards the kitchen.

Misty handed Leo the deck, she knew he preferred, and he shuffled slowly and carefully. When he was ready, he chose his cards and placed them in the appropriate spots.

Misty raised her brows and smiled. "Oh, my. You are on a whirlwind heading into the new year."

"I am?"

She nodded. "Have you met someone special? Perhaps at the golf club?"

Leo stared hard at the cards. "No. Am I going to?"

"It's inevitable." Misty winked at him. "Make sure you're ready for romance, Leo. Big things are about to happen."

"Do the cards say when?"

"No. Nothing that specific. Immediate future is all I can say with certainty."

Leo smiled. "Marvelous. I am more than ready for a new golf partner."

After watching a movie together, Misty and Angelique went upstairs to bed. At some point in the night, something woke her with a start. Hoodoo growled long and low. Misty blinked up at the ceiling wondering how long she'd been asleep. She reached for her cell on the nightstand to check the time, and it was three a.m.

"Back to sleep, Hoo. It's the middle of the night." Then Misty heard Angelique in the hallway outside her room. She got up and joined her at the top of the stairs. "What did you hear, *ma chere*?"

"Sounded like someone open de door," Angelique said. "Hoo hear something too?"

"He did, but he's fine now. Maybe just the house creaking." Misty checked the safe built into the floor in her room, and the book sat safely wrapped in its protective covering. "I'll call a security company in the morning."

Blaine wanted to do it when he was here.

I   should've   listened.

CHAPTER THREE

Monday, January 2nd.

<u>Nine Saint Gillian Street</u>

Thinking the security company she'd randomly chosen from the internet wouldn't be open because of the holiday, Misty left a message—her name and number. She needed an estimate on a system. If someone tried to break into the house, she and Angelique were at risk. It's not like she had Blaine in the bed beside her anymore. Someone who could hop up and shoot a burglar through the eye at a moment's notice.

She wrapped her black robe tightly around her and filled the kettle. No one had called for an appointment for today, so she and Angelique should make a new batch of salve while they had a moment's peace.

When the tea steeped, Angelique poured herself a cup and carried it into the front parlor to watch the early news. Life must be different for her there. There were things that living in her home offered that she'd never been able to do in the bayou with no electricity.

Misty sipped her tea, set the cup down, and wrote a list of ingredients she needed for a batch of healing salve. She'd check the pantry before calling around to suppliers to get the rest.

"Madam Misty, come," called Angelique.

Misty hurried into the front room and sat down on the sofa. The news anchor was reporting on a four-year-old boy taken from his mother's car on New Year's Day. The mother had taken her son to the convenience store two blocks from their home in north New Orleans to buy cigarettes and some snacks.

Between their house and the store, it started to rain, so she left Ryan in the SUV while she ran into the store. When she came out—she estimated it was a total of four minutes—Ryan was gone.

The mother, a young blonde girl in her late twenties, was crying on camera asking whoever took her son to bring him back. The husband, a tall man with dark-rimmed glasses, stood behind her, looking glum and saying nothing.

"Anyone with information to Ryan's whereabouts is asked to call this number," said the news anchor. A number flashed across the bottom of the screen, and Angelique wrote it down.

"What you think, Madam?"

Misty sighed. She'd tried to help before, and they'd looked at her like she was from outer space. "Let's see if they find him by tomorrow. We'll give it a day."

Misty's cell was ringing in the kitchen when she

went back to refill her teacup.

"Hi. My name is Charlotte McLean. I was wondering if you had any openings for tonight for a reading? My cousin Michele and I want to come together if we can. If that's okay."

"Sure, that's fine. My evening is free. Can you come at seven?"

"Thank you, Madam LeJeune. See you at seven."

"Customers?" asked Angelique.

Misty held up two fingers. "Two for seven o'clock."

"People anxious for de new year."

Misty was deep in thought about Ryan, the missing little boy, when her cell rang again.

"This is Linc Castille from Castille Security returning your call. How can I help you?"

"Oh perfect. I didn't realize you were working today. I wanted an estimate on a security system for my house."

There was a pause, and she heard him flipping papers. "I could come by in an hour if you're not busy or tomorrow morning around ten. Do either of those times suit you?"

"Yes, thank you. I'm home all day today. An hour will be perfect for me." She gave him the address and ended the call.

"You're not getting one of those useless security systems, are you, Mystere?" Daddy asked from the corner.

"I think I will. Why do you think they're useless?"

"The old ways are better. A gun, a knife, or a vicious spell cast against an intruder."

Misty giggled. "What if I don't wake up in time to grab my gun, my knife, or my wand?"

"Oh, you're thinking more of an early warning system?"

"The man will be here in an hour. Listen to him before you cross him off."

"Of course, I will, Mystere. I'm reasonable."

"No, you're not. You're a ghost, and a short-tempered one at that. Now let me work. Angelique and I need to get our ingredients together to make a batch of salve.

An hour later, Misty had a fresh pot of coffee on the warmer in the kitchen, and the front parlor had been tidied and dusted by Angelique yet again. The doorbell chimed, and the security man arrived.

Misty opened the door, and she felt it immediately. The warm honey dripping feeling that she felt with Blaine. Why did that feeling overcome her? Did this man put a spell on her?

She smiled as she took in the sight of him. Dark coppery skin and dark hair, extremely attractive. But those eyes—the eyes looking back at her were green like her own and full of mystery—deep pools of unfathomable danger.

"Come in. I'm Misty LeJeune."

"Lincoln Castille—call me Linc." Dressed in jeans and a black turtleneck, he stepped inside with a tan leather briefcase in his hand. "I'm pleased to meet you, Miss LeJeune. This is N'Orlean, so of course, I've heard of you and your family."

She wouldn't ask what he'd heard. A lot of rumors swirled around in N'Orlean. Misty pointed at the archway into the front parlor. "Please have a seat. Would you like coffee?"

He smiled, and she felt it again—the honey. "Please. I could use a cup. It's not the warmest day in January out there." He sat down on the sofa, placed his case on the old wooden coffee table and began spreading out brochures.

Angelique brought the coffee on a tray along with cream and sugar and a plate of ginger cookies.

"Thank you," he said to Angelique before he turned to Misty on the other side of him. "This is a large house. Do you have any idea what kind of system you want?"

"No, but I can find out from someone I know who is familiar with the house."

"Your boyfriend?"

"Some time ago, my ex-boyfriend wanted me to have a system installed. I'm sure he has ideas of what I need."

"Was the parting amicable enough for you to call him?"

"A little more amicable now than it was at first." Misty pressed Blaine's contact number. "Hey, Beb, it's me. I have a security guy here about the system. Could you talk to him?"

"Well, hallelujah. Look at you, doing something sensible. Yeah, put him on."

Linc hesitated as he took the phone. "Who am I talking to?"

"Blaine Blackmore-Powell in Texas."

Misty watched Linc's face as he listened to Blaine. Linc moved brochures around, flipped them over, nodded his head, and said "uh-huh" several times.

"Okay, I think I've got it. Thanks for your time, sir."

"Did that help?" asked Misty.

"He knows what he wants you to have."

Misty shrugged. "He's a genius."

"He sounded smart."

"No, he's a genius—a real one—and knows about crime."

"Oh." Linc raised a dark eyebrow. He sorted through all of his brochures until he selected one. "This is the system he wanted you to go with if you're comfortable with it."

Misty smiled. "Blaine wouldn't care what the price was . . . but I do. What am I looking at?"

"Well, no, he didn't care about the price. In fact, he said for me to send him the bill."

Misty smiled. "That's something he would say, but I'd rather take care of it myself if it's in my range."

"Shall I write everything out so you can see where

I'm getting the costs, and then you can decide with a little more knowledge of what I'm basing the pricing on?"

"Yes, please." She turned to Angelique. "Would you get Mr. Castille more coffee, *Chere?*"

"Of course, Madam."

Linc glanced up from his figuring. "May I say how lovely you are, Madam LeJeune?"

Misty dipped her chin. "Thank you. Nice of you to notice."

"I couldn't help it. A blind man would notice."

Hoodoo laid down next to her. Protective, but not minding the stranger too much. Nothing like his reaction to Fabian Landry. *Man, Hoo hated that one.*

Misty watched Linc write numbers, and she wanted to touch his hair. Instead, she asked, "So if the company is named Castille Security, you must be the owner?"

He looked up and smiled. "It was my father's company, but he passed away, and I'm carrying on as best I can."

"I'm sorry," said Misty. "Was it recent?"

"Last year. I'm adjusting."

"My Daddy is dead also," said Misty, "but he still lives here in the house. It's comforting."

Linc's eyes widened. "Your house is haunted?"

"No, not haunted. Only Daddy lives here. Nobody else."

Linc stopped writing numbers. "Can you see him?"

"Yes, sometimes. Mostly I hear him talking to me."

"Wow, that's hard to wrap my head around."

"Are you a non-believer?"

"No. I've just never had enough personal experience to base an opinion on."

"That was diplomatic."

Linc smiled. "I try not to offend."

Misty sat back in her chair. "I don't try. I tell it like it is and let the chips fall."

He chuckled and went back to the quote. When the numbers were added and double-checked, Linc looked up at her. "Mr. Blackmore-Powell said he preferred a monitored system. That's an additional monthly fee that has nothing to do with purchasing the system or the installation."

"Got it," said Misty. "An extra. How much a month?"

"Twenty-nine ninety-five."

"Like Netflix or something?"

"Almost, but the movie is about break-ins," said Linc.

Misty smiled. "Angelique thought she heard someone last night, but we didn't see anybody."

"Once the system is installed, I'll be able to tell if a window or door is breached. I can pinpoint exactly which one."

Misty liked that. "Do you respond in person, or do the police come?"

"Both. Did you have other problems? It's quite common for people to call for an estimate after they've had a scare."

"Mostly, it just makes sense, but there's someone I don't trust, and maybe it's bothering me a little."

"A physical threat? Someone who would do you harm?"

"More like a snooping thief. But who knows, he might also crack me over the head to get what he wants."

"I don't like the sound of that. Have you talked to the police?"

"I don't think the police would help me much."

"Then I think we should get your system installed as soon as possible. I'll see if I can send a couple of my men to start in the morning."

"Would you? Thank you so much. I know Angelique is nervous." Misty made it sound like it was her assistant who was nervous, but she was fighting a case of nerves herself.

Linc gathered up his papers and gave her a copy of the quote. "I'll need a deposit before we can begin work, then the balance when you're up and running."

"How much should I make the check out for?"

"Is five hundred in your range?"

Misty fumbled in her purse for her checkbook. After scribbling down the numbers, she handed it over. "Will you be coming with the men in the morning?"

"Yes, I'll be here first thing, then I may have to leave to go to another job."

"You sound busy."

"December was slow. It's good to have work."

After Linc left, Misty went to the kitchen and poured herself a glass of wine. "He was nice. Was he the one, Daddy?"

"He seemed like an upstanding young man."

"He did, although my reaction to him felt a little sudden. Do you think he could have hexed me?"

"I didn't feel it, Mystere. Although I'm not as sensitive as I used to be."

"What did you think, Angelique?"

Angelique had the long work table covered in bottles and jars ready for the new batch of healing salve she'd produced. "He was polite. D'at says something about his upbringing."

Misty looked over the progress of their salve project. "You got a lot done while I was talking security. I'll help you with the jars and the labels."

"Do we have orders waitin?" asked Angelique.

"There's a list. I'll find it and get the shipping supplies."

"Are you behind on orders, Mystere?" her Daddy asked.

"A little, Daddy. I shouldn't have gone to Austin. That put me behind and caused all kinds of problems for Blaine. I should have stayed here and finished my work. The cards told me to think carefully about leaving, and I didn't listen."

"You must always listen, my darling girl. The Tarot is never wrong."

She laughed at herself. "How many times a day do I tell people that, and still I chose the wrong path. Lesson learned. I'll be more careful in the future."

After supper, Misty retired into the front parlor to watch the news with Angelique.

"Look, Madam. D'at Fabian Lanrdy is on de news."

Misty turned up the volume to hear what Fabian was saying to the blonde newswoman with the pouty red lips. "I have offered my services. I believe I can assist Mr. and Mrs. Cormier in finding their son, Ryan."

"And you would do this, how, Mr. Landry?"

"Energy carries insight. Provided with articles of clothing, or a favorite toy, his whereabouts might be revealed."

"I wish *I* had something belonging to the little boy. I didn't feel more than the slightest ounce of true power from him. He's an ambulance chaser."

"I'll get you something of the boy's, Mystere."

"You can't do that, Daddy. Something might happen."

"What could happen? I'm already dead." He chuckled, and it was an eerie sound. "What's the address?"

"I have no idea. They aren't disclosing the boy's

address." Misty stood and paced for a moment. "I know what you could do, Daddy. You could follow Fabian. After the TV interview, the station will take him to talk to the parents."

"I'd better hurry. Wish me luck." Her Daddy disappeared, and Misty was left wondering what Fabian Landry was up to.

The news was wrapping up when the doorbell rang. Angelique freed herself from the sofa and brushed her skirt back into place. "That's de seven o'clock clients, Madam."

Hoodoo barked, and Misty hurried to the door. She'd forgotten about the evening appointment.

Thank the goddess for Angelique.

She pulled the heavy door open, and before her stood two young girls, both wearing winter coats and watch caps. "Come in. Y'all look cold."

The pair stepped into the grand foyer, and Misty got a wave of their expectant excitement. They were nervous and skittish, and their energy was bubbling right off them. "Let me hang up your coats, girls."

"I'll do it," said Angelique. *"Bienvenue, les filles."*

"Merci," said one of the girls to Angelique.

In the front parlor, Misty used the round oak pedestal table that used to be in the dining room before the renovations. The surface was covered with a black satin cloth to ward off any negativity during the reading of the Tarot.

"Have a seat and get comfortable," Misty said. "Let's start by you telling me your names."

The girl with long dark hair that framed a heart-shaped face waved her fingers and smiled. "I'm Charlotte McLean. I'm the one who phoned you." Charlotte looked about nineteen or twenty. A pretty face devoid of makeup, and she wore dark-rimmed glasses.

Misty picked up a vibe of apprehension from Charlotte. The girl was nervous and anxious, but it was about more than having her first Tarot reading. Maybe the cards would reveal what was bothering her.

"And how did you hear about me?" asked Misty.

"We asked people in Jackson Square," said Charlotte. "Several people told us you were the best."

"Well, isn't that flattering." Misty took the Tarot deck out of the velvet bag and shuffled. "And what's your name?"

"I'm Michele Lennox." The other girl had dark honey blonde hair and her expressive eyes told Misty that she'd seen a lot of sadness in her young life.

"Who wants to go first?"

"Michele does," said Charlotte, throwing her friend under the bus. Michele turned a shade of pale and stared at the cards in Misty's hands.

"You don't have to be frightened. Tarot cards are only a guidance system. They won't say anything to scare you. Are you ready?"

"I think so."

"Good. Let's start with what brought you in for a

SCHOOL FOR RELUCTANT WITCHES · 39

reading? Is there a question you're struggling with or something you're wondering about?"

During the readings, the girls were quiet, attentive, and almost seemed to be holding their breath. They listened to every word nodding their heads as if they agreed with what the cards had to say. They were actually, quite adorable.

After the readings, Angelique served raspberry tea and ginger cookies.

"So, what did you think?"

"That was so amazing, how you did that," said Michele, grabbing a cookie. "I want to learn how to read the cards."

"You can almost teach yourself. Buy a deck that speaks to you, most come with a little book inside."

"Do you give lessons?" asked Charlotte. "That would be so cool. I bet you'd get a lot of people who want to take them."

"No, I'm pretty busy with the healing side of my business. I make natural remedies."

"Ooh, that's amazing," said Michele.

"No, it's more like hard work. Angelique helps me."

Michele's eyes lit up. "We could help you for free if you need more hands. Couldn't we Char?"

Charlotte's head bobbed as the excitement in the room ratcheted. "Sure, we could. We're not busy."

"Don't you go to school?"

Charlotte eyed the cookies, and Misty urged her to

take another. She beamed and went for it. "We're finished school and have part-time jobs at Raising Cane."

Misty smiled. "That's a lovely offer, girls. Why don't you leave your cell numbers and I'll call if I get behind."

"You *are* behind, Madam." Angelique collected the used teacups and plates.

Misty cast Angelique a look, but the woman wasn't a bit sorry. "Okay. Maybe Angelique and I could use a hand tomorrow. I have security men coming and won't be able to help her much with the current orders."

"Oh, thank you, Madam LeJeune," said Michele. "What time should we come?"

Misty shrugged and glanced at Angelique. "Ten?"

"Ten is perfect," said Charlotte.

The girls left in a cyclone of excited chatter, and Misty wondered what she'd gotten herself into. Really though, how much trouble could they be making salves? It wasn't like she was teaching them spellcasting or anything. Just simple healing properties and labeling.

It should be fine.

The Apartment, New Orleans

Charlotte ran up the outside staircase to the tiny apartment she and Michele shared with their friend Diana. Situated above Diana's Grandmother's garage, it wasn't big, but it was theirs. Diana was sacked out in front of Netflix, as usual, waiting for their return, her spikey, black pixie cut sticking up from where she'd been lying on it. "Hey, how'd it go?"

"Di, you won't believe what just happened."

She paused her show and looked over. Diana was a couple of years younger than them, but the three of them got along like sisters. "Let me guess. Madam LeJeune told both of you that you'd marry rich, handsome men with millions of dollars."

"No, nothing like that, smarty pants." Charlotte made a face but wouldn't have her excitement squashed. "She said we could come back to help her assistant, Angelique, make healing products tomorrow."

"Cool, how much are you getting paid?"

"Well, nothing. We're doing it for free," said Michele.

Diana laughed. "Yeah, that's great news. You're giving up your free time, to make boil creams for someone else to sell, and you're getting nothing for it."

Now it was Michele's turn to frown. "Don't you see? We all go, and as soon as she knows us a little bit better, she'll teach us magick."

"I know a little magick already," said Diana. "I'm good."

"What we know isn't *real* magick. We have magick in our bodies crying to get out." Charlotte threw her coat over the back of a chair and twirled her scarf in the air. "By the end of the week, I'll be able to levitate."

"Yourself, or a tractor-trailer?" Diana giggled at the two of them and waved the clicker. "Yeah, great news.

I'm happy you're happy. What movie are we watching tonight?"

Nine Saint Gillian Street

Hours passed, and still, Misty's father hadn't returned. She and Angelique drank tea and read the Tarot until after midnight, and even then, he didn't come home.

"He's never done this before," Misty said, staring at the corner of the kitchen for the hundredth time.

"Can you call him?" asked Angelique.

"I've never tried calling a ghost. I'm not a medium."

"Try, Madam. I'm sure he'll answer you."

Misty took Angelique's hand and closed her eyes.

> *Lost spirit speak to me.*
> *Assure me you are well.*
> *I wait for your return.*
> *This my summoning spell.*

"So mote it be," they said in unison.

They waited.

Nothing.

"Either he didn't hear the call and he's not coming, or something happened and he's not coming. Any way you look at it, staying up all night isn't helping. Let's go to bed."

CHAPTER FOUR

Tuesday, January 3rd.

<u>Nine Saint Gillian Street</u>

The house felt strangely quiet when Misty woke, and the first thing she thought of was her father. "Daddy did you come home?" she asked in a whisper.

"I'm here, child, watching you sleep. Did you worry?"

"A little. I called you, and you didn't answer."

"I felt your call but was too busy to return."

"Busy doing what?"

"I got to the TV station in time to see Fabian Landry get into a vehicle with a couple of TV people."

"Did they go to Ryan's house?"

"Yes. Once they were all inside, I went in and listened."

"They didn't see you, did they?"

"Of course not. I'm the epitome of discretion."

"Did Fabian put on a big show about finding the

boy?"

"Did he ever." Daddy chuckled. "That charlatan even had me convinced he could find the child."

"No, he didn't."

"No, he didn't. I think the parents wanted to believe him, so they bought everything that man was selling. Fabian held a shirt of Ryan's in his hands and sat with his eyes closed for ever so long. Then he opened his eyes and stared straight ahead like he was deranged."

Misty giggled. "Then what?"

"Then he said he couldn't comment on what he'd seen until he had time to put the pieces together in his mind. He didn't want to cause the family any further stress until he was sure of the vision."

"Didn't they press him to reveal?"

"The TV people surely did, but the parents became tearful, and so the talk was abandoned. I think they were hoping for an exact location and a swift end to the whole terrible ordeal."

"Well, Daddy, you know where the parents live. Now I can go and see if I can help them, but not until Mr. Landry is done messing with them."

"You must move quickly, Mystere. The man who took him is dangerous. I fear he might kill the boy before the police get to him."

Misty sat up. "You know who took him? How did you figure that out?"

"I sat in mother's car—the one with the child's car seat in the back—and I saw him. He is a very bad man and left a strong residual presence."

"What did he look like, Daddy? This is important."

"Never mind what he looked like, child. Just phone the police station and give them his name."

Misty's green eyes grew wide with wonder at her father's powers. They might have diminished in death, but he was still a force to be reckoned with. "You know his name?"

"Jethro Oxcart or something like that."

Misty paused. "Oxcart? You're not sure?"

"His name impressed upon me so quickly I cannot be certain. Perhaps you could phone Blaine and have him look for a registered pedophile with a name something like that. The police have a list."

"You think he's a pedophile?"

"Sadly, I'm certain of it, my love. His aura gave off the most disturbing energies."

"My, my, Daddy. You're on fire this morning."

"I try to stay alert, but sometimes it's hard."

"I can imagine."

He laughed the eerie sounding laugh, and it made Misty shiver. "Thankfully, no, you can't."

Forgetting to check the time, Misty picked up her cell and called Blaine. "Sorry, Beb. I did it again, didn't I? I apologize for waking you."

"Misty, I'm always happy when you call. What can I do for you? Is everything all right?"

"With me, yes. But I have to ask a favor."

"Sure anything. Is it about your security system?"

"No. That's all been taken care of. Installation is starting this morning."

"I'm happy you're going ahead with that. It makes sense when you live alone. What can I help you with?"

"There is a little boy missing in the city, and Daddy thinks a pedophile took him."

"Your father said that?"

"Yes. He thinks the man's name is something like Jethro Oxcart. Is there a list you can look at before I call the police and look like an idiot?"

"There is a registry, although he may not be on it. Give me a few minutes, and I'll call you back."

"Thanks, Beb."

Misty ended the call, and the front door buzzed. "Can you get that Angelique? I'm not dressed."

"Oui, Madam."

Misty checked the time and ran into the shower. "I didn't realize those guys would be so early."

Misty's hair was still damp as she hurried downstairs to see what was happening. She hadn't even had a cup of tea, and her house was swarming with people. Not people—men. A lot of good looking men in dark blue uniforms. She scanned the crowd and didn't see Linc. Maybe he'd come later.

"Do whatever y'all need to do. I'll be in the kitchen."

The men were already going about their business and didn't seem to hear her. She entered the kitchen, and Angelique had tea brewing in the pot and a pan of bacon on the burner of the big black stove.

"That smells good. I'm hungry this morning." She filled a cup with hot tea and sat down at the table. "How far behind are we on the orders?"

"Very far, Madam. We need to *travail.*"

"The girls can help when they arrive." She took another sip of her tea, and the phone rang. "Blaine?"

"There is a man registered in the New Orleans area by the name of Jeremy Oxford. He's on parole. I'm sending the info to your cell."

"Thanks, Beb."

"Are you helping the police on a kidnapping?"

"They didn't ask me, but Daddy accidentally found out who took the boy, and I thought I should tell them."

"If they give you trouble when you call or treat your gift lightly, tell me. I won't let the police discount your input or treat you rudely. I'll take care of it."

"Thanks, sweetie. I love you for always."

"Me too, Mist. Can't help myself."

Misty wiped away a tear as she picked up her fork to eat the breakfast Angelique had cooked for her.

"Did he tell you de name of de bad man?"

"Yes. I need to write it down before I forget."

Angelique jumped up and grabbed a notepad and pen from the desk drawer. Misty printed the name Blaine had given her.

Jeremy Oxford.

The doorbell rang again, and Angelique was on her feet. "Eat, Madam. I'll get it."

Misty gave her last piece of bacon to Hoo, her lunky Bernese drooling beside her. She wiped her mouth on a napkin just in time. Linc moved into the doorway, looking hot in one of those blue uniforms, and an easy N'Oleans smile on his face.

She gestured to the table ahead of her. "Hey, would you like some coffee?"

"Love some. First, I'd better check and see if everything is going smoothly."

Misty nodded. She reached for her cell and took a deep breath. The police were going to think she was a crank, and they already had Fabian, the faker, to contend with. They'd think she was just more of the same.

Maybe I shouldn't call.

"You have to call Mystere. It's the right thing to do."

Misty jumped when her father spoke. He hadn't shown himself, and she didn't know he was in the kitchen. "Okay, but you know what they're like. They won't believe me."

"A pox on their house. All we can do is try."

Misty called and asked for the detective working on Ryan Cormier's case.

"Detective Brady Ellis, how can I help you?"

"Detective Ellis, this is Misty LeJeune calling. I may be able to help you find Ryan. I know who took him."

"You do? What did you say your name was again?"

"Mystere LeJeune. I'm a psychic, and I've worked with the police before on occasion."

The scoff on the other end of the line was muffled but she caught it. "Bad enough the family brought on Landry. Now you people are coming out of the woodwork?"

"It might seem like that, but I have information that may be helpful."

"How did you get this information, Miss LeJeune?"

"Umm… you could call it a vision."

"I'm afraid police work is about real-world investigation. Every moment I spend listening to people like you are minutes I'm not focused on doing my job."

"Wait! His name is—" Despite her trying to spit it out before Detective Ellis hung up, the call dropped before she could convey the information. She looked up at Angelique and shook her head. "He didn't believe me."

"Il est un abruti."

Misty sighed. "You're right. He *was* an asshole."

The doorbell rang again, and Angelique was on the move. For a large woman, she was amazingly quick on her feet. She returned to the kitchen moments later with Michele and Charlotte in tow.

"Aw, my eager beavers are here to help. Just in time. We have mountains of work to do."

"There are a lot of men here," said Michele.

"I'm having a security system installed. Hopefully, they won't bother us."

"Are we going to do magick today?" asked Charlotte.

"Only the magick of healing. That's most of what I do. Try to help people using the things nature gave us."

"I will get de girls started," said Angelique, handing them each an apron.

Linc stuck his head in the kitchen. "Can I see you for a minute, Misty?"

"Sure."

Linc led her into the hallway, and he pointed at the stairs with his notebook. "Can we take a look at the third floor? I need to count how many windows we need to arm and don't know how to get up there."

"Of course, I'll show you." Misty led the way up the stairs, then pointed to the narrow door in the middle of the second-floor hallway. She opened the door and wrinkled up her nose.

Eww, It smells musty up there.

She trudged up the steep steps and stood on the landing at the top. "Here we are. The third floor is divided into two huge rooms that aren't used at the moment."

"I just need to count the windows," said Linc.

"Let's see," said Misty. She stepped into the room on her right and looked around. She hadn't been up here for ages and had forgotten how much light poured in.

The space was bright and inviting, despite the stacks of old family trunks, boxes, and furniture piled in every direction.

Linc checked the windows and noted things in his notebook. "Is the other room the same as this one?"

"Pretty much, I think. I honestly haven't been up here in years." They walked across the landing into the other room, and Linc did his window count again. "It feels neglected up here. I've renovated most of the house but haven't done a thing up here on the third floor."

"Why would you if you don't need the space?" asked Linc.

Misty shrugged. "I suppose you're right."

"Besides, you seem busy enough already. You've got quite an assembly line of production going on down there. Your girls seem like they love the work."

Misty laughed. "It's their first day. They want me to teach them magick, but they're making salves. I'm sure their enthusiasm will fade."

"Are you going to teach them?"

"I don't teach. Magick is something shared amongst my family. I don't put it out for the world to see."

"Don't sell yourself short." Linc smiled, leaning a little closer. "Every time I'm near you, it feels like magick to me."

Ha. She might be in a dry spell with men, but she didn't miss the come on. "Is that your go-to line?"

"A brand new one. I just thought of it."

"I like it."

"Maybe I could take you to dinner."

Misty liked the idea, but too much was happening in her house at that moment to make plans. "We can talk about it when you take a break."

"*Madam*," Angelique hollered from the bottom of the first-floor stairs. "People here to see you."

"Coming down."

When Misty reached the second floor, Angelique leaned and whispered. "It's de police."

"Police? Why are they here?"

"*Je ne sais pas.*"

Two men in suits stood in the foyer, watching the blue uniforms at work. She went over to greet them. "Gentlemen, what can I do for y'all?"

A large black man in his late forties dipped his chin and offered her a kind smile. "I am Lieutenant White, Madam LeJeune. You called Detective Ellis this morning and said you had information about Ryan Cormier?"

When he gestured to the other officer, the man frowned like he was a naughty boy that had been disciplined by the principal. "I did, but Detective Ellis was rude and hung up on me. He said he had no time to waste speaking with me."

Lieutenant White frowned and sent the other officer a reproachful glare. "I wish to apologize for Detective Ellis, on behalf of the department. He had no knowledge of the highly respected position you and your family hold in New Orleans."

Lieutenant White had a kind voice and a gentle manner. Misty liked him right away. Ellis was shorter, sandy brown hair and a day's scruff on his face. During White's apology, Ellis hung his head and admired the foyer floor.

"We won't take much of your time, Madam," White said. "Is there someplace quiet we could talk?"

She glanced around the current chaos of her home. "Private, I can do. Quiet, I'm not so sure. I'm having a system installed as you can see, and the house is busy. My assistants are working in the kitchen, so we'll have to use the sitting room at the back of the house. Would you care for coffee?"

"No thank you," said White.

Misty showed them into the newly renovated sitting room, and they were the first to sit on the gray leather loveseats. Misty sat down opposite them in a burgundy wing chair.

The Lieutenant pulled a brown leather notebook out of his jacket pocket along with a pen. "Tell me how you happened upon this information, Madam LeJeune."

"I happened to see Fabian Landry on the news with the child's parents, yesterday. I've met Mr. Landry twice, but don't know him well."

"Do you think he's legitimate?"

Misty wasn't sure how to answer that. "I cannot say. I'm not familiar with his parentage. As a rule, magick travels from the roots of strong bloodlines. While I have never heard of the Landry's, that certainly doesn't mean anything conclusive."

White nodded and seemed to sense her hesitation. "All right. Given that you can't say for certain, do you *feel* he has psychic powers?"

No. Not a bit. "I'm sorry. I met him twice and have no idea of his prowess. He told me he helped the police in the past."

"I'm not aware of that," said Lieutenant White. "I'd love to hear what you have to say about the child, Madam LeJeune, if you would share it with us."

She drew a breath and nodded. White seemed genuinely welcoming of the information, so, of course, she wanted to help. "When I saw the boy's parents on the television, I wanted, like all viewers, to see the boy safely home. You might say, I sent that intention out into the world, and it came back to me with the answers I sought."

White's eyes widened. "You mean you know who took the child?"

Misty nodded. "I believe you need to focus on a man named Jeremy Oxford. He is a known pedophile on parole, and if I'm right, he is the man who took Ryan."

"We've been checking the registered offenders one by one, Madam," said Lieutenant White, "but it is an arduous and slow process. This will help us tremendously."

"And how did this information come to you, again?" Detective Ellis asked with a sneer curling his lip.

"I could never explain the workings of my craft to a

non-believer such as yourself, Detective Ellis. Believe me or not, the information came to me via a powerful magickal source."

Thanks, Daddy.

The Lieutenant nodded, and Ellis rolled his eyes.

"That's all I have for you this morning, detectives. Follow my recommendation, and you will either prove me right or wrong." She turned her attention squarely on Ellis. "But don't let a personal prejudice against magick put a boy's life at risk."

Ellis stiffened. "I'm not prejudiced. I simply don't believe in a cosmic, mystical power influencing our lives."

Misty pointed to the gold crucifix hanging around his neck. "Don't you?"

Before he had a chance to come back at her, Misty stood to escort them out. "If you wish me to help you further, I'm, of course, available to do what I can."

"If we brought you an article of Ryan's clothing like Mr. Landry said, would that help?"

"Well, yes, but I certainly wouldn't want to offend Mr. Landry or cast doubt on his credibility by stepping in."

White shook off her words. "Egos shouldn't come into play. The important thing is Ryan's safe return. I'll be back with what you need within the hour, Madam. And despite the previous impression you were given—" He cast a glare at Ellis. "—the department *is* grateful for your help."

Less than an hour later, Lieutenant White and Detective Ellis returned from the Cormier residence. The Lieutenant carried a tote bag and offered it to Misty in the foyer.

"Thank you, Lieutenant. I hope I can help you find him." Misty led the way past several men working on phases of her system, and as she passed the kitchen door she motioned to Angelique.

"Are we allowed to watch you do this, Madam?" asked Lieutenant White. "Or is privacy what you require?"

"You may watch, but I won't appreciate publicity or any mention of my participation in the solving of your case."

"I understand," said White. "You're at the opposite end of the spectrum from Mr. Landry. He seems to love being the center of attention."

"Any news there?" she asked.

Lieutenant White shook his head. "Not that I've heard."

While Misty removed the items from the tote bag— a fuzzy teddy bear, a storybook with worn pages, and a child-size Saint's ballcap—Angelique and the two girls joined her and the detectives in the parlor.

"Sit beside me, girls." Misty felt the fledgling energy in them and wondered how much magick they possessed. *I want you to remain quiet, but relaxed and focused.*

Angelique placed a glass of water on the coffee table and looked at the girls. "Madam becomes weak after a vision. We must be prepared."

Ellis stared, his attitude obvious. He'd already decided she was a fake and was waiting to tear her down. He'd be sorry. She'd see to it.

"We checked the last known address for Jeremy Oxford," said Lieutenant White. "He wasn't there, and the canvas of the street turned up nothing. No one has seen him in his old neighborhood since he was released on parole."

Misty worried that with a man like Oxford, Ryan might already be lost to them. "Then let us do our best to bring him home, shall we?"

Charlotte and Michele sat close to her, eyes wide.

Misty drew a deep breath and picked up the teddy bear. Holding it close to her heart, a wave of fear and longing overtook her almost immediately. She brushed at the tears warming her cheek. "Ryan misses his teddy. He can't sleep without Mr. Bumble Bear."

When she'd spent enough time reaching out for information, she set the bear on the table and let out a sigh.

"What do you need, Madam?" asked Angelique.

"Hot tea and something sweet, please. I feel faint."

Angelique left the room, and Misty trained her gaze on Lieutenant White. "Ryan is in a dark room. He's tied to a bed—more like a cot—and he's crying."

"You saw that?" asked White.

"Flashes of it. I only see flashes. Like a movie with pieces missing. I have to sort it out."

Angelique brought the tea and placed it on the table. Misty picked up the cup with a trembling hand and took a couple of sips. Then she set the cup down and held the hands of both girls. "We're doing well. Did you feel the energy?"

"When you held the teddy bear, I felt so sad." Michele pressed a hand against her t-shirt and rubbed her chest.

"I wanted to cry," said Charlotte.

"Let's try the book," said Misty. She took a sip of tea, then picked up the book and held it in both hands. She groaned, hating the feeling of hopeless fear twisting her insides. "Trailer. Dirty trailer. Dogs running. River. A sign. I see the sign."

Angelique wrote everything down.

Misty slumped back against the sofa cushions and tried to catch her breath. "May I have your pen, Angelique? I saw a sign at the gate of a trailer park."

"Ryan is being held in a trailer park?" asked White. "Any idea where?"

Misty shook her head as she printed letters on the notepad. "I think this is what it said, but I have no idea where it is." She handed White the note.

"Thibodeaux."

Lieutenant White had his cell phone in his hand. "I'm Googling the name of the trailer park, Madam, to see if I can get an address."

Misty nodded.

Charlotte gently placed Ryan's things back in the tote bag.

"I have it," said the Lieutenant. "There is a trailer park by that name just outside of town. I can't thank you enough, Madam LeJeune."

"Will you call if you find him?"

"Yes, definitely."

Charlotte offered the bag to Detective Ellis. "Take his teddy to him, sir. He misses him so much."

The two men rushed to the door, and Misty followed. She pulled the curtain back, peeked through the sidelight, and concentrated hard on Detective Ellis's shoelaces.

Hurrying to keep up with his boss, Ellis tripped and fell on the flagstone walk. He stood up, cursing and brushing the dirt from his pants.

Misty giggled and returned to the girls in the kitchen.

"That was amazing." Michele pressed her hands to her cheeks and jumped up and down, her blonde ponytail swinging wildly. "Oh, there is so much I need to learn."

Misty smiled. "It takes years and many hours of practice."

"But you could teach us," Charlotte said, sending her a pleading look. "Pleeeease?"

Misty was torn. "I'm not sure I want the responsibility that comes with teaching others. Magick can be a wonderful gift but can also be dangerous if not respected."

"Oh, no," Charlotte said, holding up her palm as if taking an oath. "We would respect the heck out of everything you say and take it very seriously."

Misty had to give them credit. They talked a good game. "I'll think about it. First we must catch up on the orders."

"We'll come back tomorrow and work extra hard," said Michele. "I promise."

The girls left for home at the same time the security men packed up their tools. "We're finished for today," said Linc. "I think we can wrap up tomorrow, then we'll test the system, and I'll show you how to use it."

"Will you stay for a drink? I'm pouring myself a glass of wine. Would you like one? Beer maybe?"

"Thanks. Yeah, I could use a beer. Were you able to help the police?"

"Possibly. They promised to call." She led the way into the kitchen and opened the fridge. "I only have Corona."

"That's fine. I'm not fussy."

"I am," said Misty as she selected a bottle from the cooler. She pointed at a chair, and Linc sat down at the ten-foot worktable. "Tell me all about Linc, the person."

"Okay, what's the abbreviated version? I'm single, thirty-two, work too much, and don't have time for a social life."

"Uh-huh. What music do you like?" asked Misty.

"Jazz and blues. Zydeco, if I'm in a party mood, but that hardly ever happens."

Misty giggled and sipped her wine.

Angelique began cooking dinner, and Misty asked Linc to stay. "What are you making, *ma chere*?"

"Fried catfish and cornbread."

"Tres bon."

"I love catfish," said Linc, agreeing to stay. "There is one place downtown that I go sometimes. The food is so good. I always end up overeating. I'll take you there."

"Are we going on a date?"

"If you ever did me the honor."

"How formal. I'd be delighted to go to dinner with you."

"How about Friday night?"

"Friday will be perfect. Thank you."

The Apartment. New Orleans.

Charlotte and Michele were pumped as they changed into their uniforms for work. "We had so much fun today, Diana. You wouldn't believe the stuff we learned just by being in that house and hanging with Madam LeJeune.

"You should come with us," said Michele. "We're going to ask her again to teach us stuff."

"Is she nice?"

"We get to call her Misty, and she's nice and so powerful. She floats when she walks, her feet barely touch the floor."

Diana raised an eyebrow. "I'm not buying that."

"Then, you'll have to come see it for yourself."

Nine Saint Gillian Street

Linc left shortly after dinner, and Misty was in good spirits as she helped Angelique clean up the kitchen. When her cell rang, she answered it, hoping that her good fortune continued.

"Madam, this is Lieutenant White. We found the boy. He's frightened and upset of course. There's no telling what Oxford did to him, yet, but he's not dead, thanks to you."

"I was happy to help, sir."

"May I call you in the future, Madam?"

"If I can be of assistance, feel free to come to me." She ended the call and smiled at Angelique. "They found him."

"Poor little boy."

"You can expect a call from Fabian Landry," said a voice from the corner of the room. "He won't be pleased that you stepped into his limelight."

"Are you guessing, Daddy? Or predicting?"

"Take your pick, Mystere."

CHAPTER FIVE

Wednesday, January 4th.

<u>Nine Saint Gillian Street</u>

At nine o'clock the next morning, Linc Castille showed up with his men. "We should finish by noon, Misty, and as soon as everything is completed and tested, I'll give you a short lesson on how to operate the system."

"Call me when y'all are ready. I'll be in the kitchen."

Holding a thick black candle in her hand, Angelique wore a perplexed look on her beautiful face when Misty reached the kitchen. "What is it, *ma chere*?"

"I need de words for de candle spell to put protection on de house when d'ey finish."

"Uh-huh. I'll get the book for you."

"But Madam, de men might see," said Angelique. "We should wait."

"I don't think any of Linc's men are interested in the LeJeune Book of Shadows." As soon as she spoke the words, Fabian Landry called.

"We need to talk, Misty."

"No. I don't think we do, Fabian."

"I know you found the boy. You made me look like a phony, and I'm not. I *do* have power, maybe not as keenly developed as yours, but I'm not a fake. Why can't we work together? We would make an amazing team."

"I work alone," said Misty.

Not totally alone. I have Daddy.

"I'd like to pop over and present you with a proposition."

"I'll save you the trouble. I'm not interested," said Misty. "Please don't come to my house. I won't let you in."

"My, aren't you the nasty witch."

Misty sighed. "I can be anything I need to be to fit the circumstances. You've put me on the defensive, Fabian."

"I'm not afraid of your power," said Fabian, "I have plenty of my own."

You have no idea of my power.

Linc walked into the kitchen as she ended the call. "Sorry, did I interrupt? You don't look happy."

"An annoyance. Let's not give him another thought."

"If you have a minute, I'd like to show you the panel in the foyer and explain how it works."

Misty turned to Angelique. "I'll get what you need in a few minutes."

Linc shook his head. "Go ahead and get Angelique what she wants. I can wait."

"Okay," said Misty. "All right. It will only take a minute." She ran up the stairs and into her room to retrieve the Book of Shadows. She opened the safe and was about to lift the book out of its hiding place when her father spoke and startled her. "There is danger in the house, my child. Do not reveal the book at this time."

Misty trembled. "Who, Daddy. Who is the danger?"

He was gone, and she didn't know what to do. Should she put it back in the safe or take it down to the kitchen to Angelique? Who could the danger be?

Is Daddy wrong?

The doorbell rang, and that decided the matter.

Misty tucked the book back into its hiding place and twirled the dial on the safe. As she descended the stairs, she could hear Angelique talking to Charlotte and Michele.

"We brought Diana with us today," said Charlotte. "She's a hard worker, and she has gifts too."

Misty welcomed the three, taking in the energy of the newcomer. "We all have gifts. Some more obvious than others. We simply learn how to use what the goddess has bestowed."

"Diana can see things in the tea leaves," said Michele.

Diana looked a couple of years younger than the other two. Her black hair was short and spikey, and her aura was bright yellow. A spiritual girl.

Misty smiled, wondering what in the world she'd do with all these young girls. She turned, and Linc stood in the kitchen doorway watching her. "Oh, I forgot about the panel lesson. I'm coming right now."

He nodded. Something about his eyes caught her attention.

Daddy is making me paranoid.

Now she was wary of everyone.

After lengthy instruction on the workings of the new system, Linc left with promises to call her about their dinner date on Friday.

I haven't been on a date for a long while.

At two-thirty, Misty changed into one of the long flowing dresses she wore when customers came for Tarot readings. The one she chose for today was yellow, with shimmers of orange through it. Happy and uplifting. She fixed her makeup and brushed her hair before venturing back downstairs. She glanced at the floor as she left the room and realized she still hadn't got the Book of Shadows out of its safe place for Angelique.

I'll do it when there's no one here.

Misty descended the staircase and headed to the kitchen, thinking she had time to relax a moment before clients arrived.

"Oh, Madam LeJeune," Charlotte said, wonder widening her chestnut eyes. "You look so pretty. I love your hair."

"Thank you, sweetie. And remember, you girls may

call me Misty. It would make things a lot easier."

"Okay," said Michele. "May we sit in the front parlor while you do the readings? We won't make a sound."

Angelique shook her head, obviously wary of the idea.

Misty wasn't sure either but had grown up watching her father and knew how much she'd gleaned simply from being present. "We can try it, but if your presence disturbs the energy or bothers the clients, I'll give you a signal, and you'll need to excuse yourselves."

Charlotte flashed a beautiful smile. "Okay. Deal."

Just after three o'clock, four ladies in their late fifties visiting New Orleans for the first time showed up at the door for their appointment. Angelique welcomed them into the foyer, took their coats, and showed them into the front parlor.

"We're so excited you fit us in, Madam LeJeune. We've had several readings in Jackson Square already. We're on a bus trip from Ohio, and are having so much fun."

The other three women were gossiping and laughing and all talking at once.

"Have y'all experienced our fabulous restaurants?" asked Misty in her slow drawl. "N'Orlean has wonderful food."

"We've tried several," said another woman. "Wonderful food, but the bakeries . . . Goodness, how I love the bakeries."

So did Blaine.

Misty fought the ache of missing him and stayed focused. "Let's get y'all settled around the table, and then we'll start the readings. One at a time."

Angelique served tea and cookies after the reading. She collected the money from the ladies and took it to the cash box in the kitchen to put it away.

After the ladies departed, the three girls reluctantly took their coats from the closet and accepted it was time for them to leave. "That was amazing, Misty," Charlotte said. "I want to be a witch, just like you."

After dinner, when the house was still, Misty took the Book of Shadows from its hiding place in her bedroom and brought it down to the kitchen. She thumbed through the worn and brittle pages until she found the protection spell Angelique wanted to use on the new security system.

"Here you are, *Chere.*" Misty traced the inked lettering dancing across the old, pressed paper, and smiled at the tingle caressing her skin. "Do you want to write it down?"

Angelique copied the spell, and before she could start casting the protection, the doorbell rang.

Misty shook her head. "No. No more company today."

"I'll send d'em off," said Angelique.

Misty stuck her head out the kitchen door and

listened to hear Angelique at the front of the house. She was tired from giving those four readings at once and didn't have the energy for any more bother.

"Mr. Landy. Madam is no receivin any more guest today."

She told him *not* to come. Deceit was one thing, disrespect and violating her wishes was quite another.

Misty didn't like Angelique facing Fabian Landry on her own and headed down the hall from the kitchen. She turned the corner in time to see him push into the foyer.

He knocked Angelique with a rough hand and sent her stumbling back against the antique half-moon table. The poor dear lost her balance and fell, taking the hall table down with her. The vase of flowers crashed onto the marble floor beside her. Shards of glass, flowers, and water scattered and splashed across the foyer floor.

Misty sprinted down the hall, fury firing her blood, and her hand retrieving her father's wand from her pocket.

> *Goddess of the bayou, Queen of the bog*
> *Turn the false one with eye of a dog*
> *Forever to croak and squat on a log*
> *Fabian Landry become a frog*

Pointing the wand, energy erupted from within and shot from her body, through her arm, and out through her fingers. The jolt of light arced across the foyer, hitting Fabian Landry right between his beady eyes.

Magick snapped in the smoke-filled foyer, and when it cleared, a sizeable green frog sat in the middle of the mess on the marble floor.

Ribbet.

Misty giggled and let her arm fall back to her side.

"T'ank you, Madam," said Angelique, her eyes wide.

Misty helped her friend to her feet and picked a couple of glass bits out of Angelique's long black hair.

"I get de mop and clean up dis mess."

"First we should take Fabian out to the garden," said Misty staring down at the fat frog. "He's slimy, and I don't want to touch him."

"We toss him in a bucket."

The silver-green shimmer of her father appeared in the doorway of the front parlor. "Mystere, what have you done now, my darling?"

"I didn't mean to, Daddy. I told him not to come here." She pointed at the upended table. "Look what he did, pushing in here like a brute. He could've hurt Angelique knocking her over as he did. Luckily she wasn't cut by broken glass."

"Then he deserved what he got, did he?"

"I think so. He was a slimy man, and now he'll be slimy ever after." Misty peeked out at the red car parked at the curb. "What about his car, Daddy? People will know he was here."

"Let me ponder it. I'll think of a solution."

Angelique returned with the mop and an empty blue bucket. She made a face as she reached down with both hands and picked Fabian up. Slimy as he was, he slipped out of her grasp and plopped into the bucket.

Ribbet. Ribbet.

Angelique laughed and couldn't seem to stop. *"Tres drole*, Madam."

Misty got laughing too. "Let's toss him in the garden, and while we're outside, we'll thank the goddess of the bayou for her help."

Angelique followed Misty out the back door and through the sunporch into the generous garden area behind the huge house. "Where do you want him, Madam?"

"Near the fishpond, I guess. He might like to swim."

Angelique turned the bucket over, and Fabian plopped into the grass near the pond.

Ribbet.

"Look at that. He thanked you, Angelique."

Angelique laughed so hard she wiped tears from her eyes.

Misty stood in the middle of the yard. She raised her arms into the air and gave thanks to the goddess of the swamp for all her many blessings and her endless love and support.

Back in the kitchen, Angelique made them both dinner, and while it cooked, they worked on the protection spell to bless the new security system.

"What did you do with Fabian the frog, Mystere?" asked the voice from the corner of the room.

"Put him in the garden, where he'll be happy. Have you thought about his car?"

"I have. Call those people who drive your car when you've been imbibing heavily. They can take his car back to his home."

"Do we have the keys?"

"*Oui*," said Angelique, pointing out toward the hallway. "His clothes dropped in a pile when he transformed."

Misty giggled. "Good. That's settled. After we deal with the car, I have to get rid of his clothes and wallet."

"We could burn d'em in de fireplace," Angelique offered.

Misty nodded. "A wonderful idea."

After dinner, Misty called one of the services listed in the yellow pages and booked a driver for the car. The young man arrived fifteen minutes later, and Misty provided him with the keys and Fabian's home address.

"Will I notify anyone when I arrive?" asked the driver.

"No. I doubt anyone will be home. The last I heard, the owner was partying hard on Bourbon Street. Just put his keys in the mailbox." She paid the man and tipped him.

"Is it time for our evening fire, Angelique? Do we have any kindling?"

Angelique checked the kindling basket next to the

fireplace and nodded. She crumpled a couple of pages of the New Orleans daily paper and made a lovely roaring fire in the hearth. Once it burned hot and steady, piece by piece, they incinerated Fabian's clothing.

Misty made a face when she tossed in Fabian's boxers covered in pictures of Homer Simpson. "What a loser."

All that remained was Fabian's wallet.

"We can't burn d'is. The leather will stink."

Misty took the cards and money out of the brown leather wallet and spread the contents on the coffee table. "Scissors, *ma chere*. I'll cut up all the cards, and we'll toss the pieces and his wallet into the trash. We can donate the cash to one of the local charities tomorrow at the grocery store."

With the burning out of the way, Misty followed her notes and set the alarm in the newly mopped foyer. Angelique lit the black candle she'd placed on the altar in the front parlor, and Misty recited the words of the protection spell three times.

> *Doers of evil stay away*
> *From my house every day*
> *Guard us always*
> *Do not stray*
> *So mote it be*

Feeling safe and secure, Misty tucked the Book of Shadows under her arm and went upstairs to bed.

CHAPTER SIX

Thursday, January 5th.

<u>Nine Saint Gillian Street</u>

Misty's sleeping brain heard the incessant ringing, but she didn't want to wake up. She was having the nicest dream about wheat fields and horses and warm summer Texas breezes. And then, there was Blaine.

"Mystere, answer your phone. Your mother is calling."

"Don't you ever sleep, Daddy?" Misty mumbled, reaching toward the nightstand. Grasping her cell, she unplugged the charger and accepted the call. "Mother, why are you calling so early? Are you all right?"

"Of course, Mystere. I'm fine. In fact, I'm more than fine. I'm flying down to N'Orlean later today to meet an important client. I thought I'd stay with you for a week, and catch up."

Misty ran a hand over her face and forced herself to wake up. "What time are you landing? I'll pick you up."

"I'm at the airport in Buffalo now, so I should be

there around one o'clock."

She nodded, excited at the prospect of her mother's visit. Things had been chaotic, and she could use a helping hand.

"Can't wait to see you, sweetheart."

"You too. See you soon, Mother." Misty tossed the duvet off and bounced out of bed.

"Claire is coming today?"

"She's on her way, Daddy. And I want you on your best behavior while she's here. You know how she hates your bad jokes."

Her father laughed. "What can she do to me?"

Misty hoped they wouldn't find out. Her father was still bitter that his wife chose to move on and move out. But he was dead. What did he expect her to do?

Angelique had a pot of tea steeping when Misty arrived in the kitchen. She poured two cups and pointed out the window. "He just sits, staring at d'at fishpond."

"Better than staring at us. He'll get used to it." Misty fished in the desk drawer for paper and pen and began making a list. "Mother is coming today, *ma chere*. We must shop and bake and make a big pot of Jambalaya."

Angelique nodded, looking nervous. "Claire LeJeune is a powerful witch. I fear her."

Misty smiled. "Don't fear her. I'll always protect you. Besides, once she sees how much you mean to me and how much you help me, she'll love you."

"How long will she remain?" asked Angelique.

"A week."

"She's staying a whole week, Mystere?" asked her father. "That won't be pleasant."

"It will be pleasant enough if you don't annoy her. Try to remember how much you loved her when you were alive."

"And how the minute I died, she moved out of the house and left me here alone? Should I forget that?"

"She moved because she couldn't bear to live here without you. Cut her some slack, Daddy."

Her father huffed. "Likely not. I find that since my untimely murder, I've become somewhat judgmental."

"Don't I know it." Misty walked to the window to peek out at Fabian frog. "He's not beside the pond. I wonder where he hopped off to?"

"We should take him to de bayou," said Angelique. "He might make some friends."

"Next time we go to Houma, we'll take him and drop him off in the swamp."

Angelique raised her dark brows. "There's many snakes and gators in de swamp. He may not last long in de wilds."

As she finished writing her list, Misty pictured a gator gobbling up Fabian Landry and nope, it didn't change her mind. That man abused Angelique and disrespected her and her family. He got what he deserved.

Her cell rang, and her smile grew. "Good morning,

Linc."

"Just checking to see if you had any trouble setting the alarm on the system. Did it work smoothly for you?"

"Yes, thank you. I'll soon have the code memorized."

"When I was leaving, I noticed Fabian Landry's red car turning your corner. Did he happen to pay you a visit? He didn't cause you any problems, did he?"

The hackles went up at the nape of Misty's neck.

Lie. "None at all," she said, as evenly as she could muster.

"Good to hear. Listen, what time should I pick you up tomorrow night?"

Misty sighed. "I'm sorry, but I have to cancel. My mother called this morning, and she's flying down today from Lily Dale. She's going to be spending some time with me."

He didn't respond, so Misty continued. "I'm picking her up this afternoon, so my free time is spoken for over the next little while. I apologize."

"I can't say I'm not disappointed. Maybe another time."

"Yes, another time." Misty frowned as she ended the call.

"What is it, Madam?"

"Linc said he passed Fabian Landry's car yesterday when he left here. He asked if he caused me any trouble."

Angelique shook her head. "*Non*. Mr. Landy come much later in de day."

"Why would Linc lie?"

Angelique shrugged. "*Je ne sais pas*."

Misty exhaled. "Damn. I liked him, too. Daddy and I thought he might be the one we called."

Her father materialized in the corner. "Maybe he saw a red car and thought it was Fabian, Mystere. Perhaps it wasn't a lie as such."

"You're defending him, Daddy?"

He held up his palms. "I believe I'll retire to the third floor and relax before your mother arrives."

Misty giggled. "You don't want to admit you were wrong about Linc Castille."

A cold wind blew through the kitchen, and he was gone.

Angelique was cracking the whip over Charlotte, Michele, and Diana when Misty returned from the airport with her mother. With black aprons wrapped around their slim bodies, they were packing boxes and taping them for shipping.

"This is quite an assembly line y'all have here." Misty's mother said. One thing was for sure, Claire LeJeune hadn't lost her Louisiana drawl living in upper New York State. At fifty-four, she was a beautiful woman. With her perfect skin and dark wavy hair, she should have been a model. Then again, Misty couldn't imagine her being anything other than a witch.

"The girls like to help," said Misty, smiling over at their eager faces. "They're hoping I'll teach them a few things."

"We must always encourage young talent," her mother said. She asked each of the girls their names and then moved closer. "Tell me what your special gift is, Diana."

"I read tea leaves."

"Interesting. I've never held an affinity for that myself. You'll have to give me a lesson. How about you, Charlotte?"

Charlotte blinked and pushed her glasses higher. "I have intuition and visions sometimes, but I don't know what they mean or where they come from."

Her mother nodded. "I can help you train your mind. That is something I know a lot about."

She pointed at Michele. "You next."

"I'm not sure what I do best, but I'm sure this is where I belong. I have to learn from Misty. It's my destiny."

Her mother accepted that with the same certainty Michele said it with. "We all have destinies mapped out by the Fates. Sometimes the path is clear, and other times our true calling is clouded by worldly claptrap. To fulfill our potential, we must rid ourselves of the useless bits."

"Would you teach us how to do that, Madam LeJeune?" asked Michele. "We would be so grateful."

"I'm only staying for a week, but I'll see what I can

do in that space of time."

"Thank you so much."

Misty smiled. Her mother loved an audience and loved to be adored. The girls were exactly the welcome she needed. Misty could already see her mother's creative wheels turning. "I'll start y'all off with homework. Tonight, write me a letter and tell me why each of y'all wants to be a witch. Agreed?"

"Ooh, yes. We can do that," said Diana.

"Mother, would you like a—"

Diana let loose with an ear-piercing scream.

Misty rushed over. "Goddess sake, what is it?"

Diana pointed at the window. "There's a huge frog on the windowsill. He's glaring at us with scary frog eyes."

"Ooh, dear." Misty tapped on the glass and shooed him off. "Get away froggy. Go for a swim."

"Maybe he's just lonely out there," Charlotte suggested. "We should name him."

Misty giggled. "He's not a pet. He doesn't need a name."

Angelique fussed over setting out a fresh snack plate. She looked like she might start laughing, and Misty couldn't look at her, or she knew she'd start too.

Michele stood on her toes to look down into the garden. "Maybe he used to be a prince. Let's name him Prince."

Misty frowned. "No. That one was never a prince. I

know that for certain." *He was a sorry excuse, wannabe psychic.*

"Let's call him Wannabe."

Charlotte giggled. "That's a funny name. I like it."

"Now that he has a name, one of you girls go out and put Wannabe at the back of the garden near the fishpond."

"Ooh, he looks slimy," said Diana.

"Go on. None of us want him making scary frog eyes at us while we're working."

The girls agreed and ran out the back door.

As soon as they were gone, her father appeared in the corner of the kitchen. "Good afternoon, my love."

Her mother tipped her head. "Hello, Josiah. Misty said you were still here. I'm thankful you're watching over our girl."

"I'm on a twenty-four-hour watch, but I don't know how useful I'd be in a crisis."

Thankfully, her mother took that moment to be kind instead of cutting. "You have more power dead than many witches who are breathing, sweetheart. I have every faith in you and always have."

"Thank you, darling," he said, obviously surprised. "That was sweet, and makes me feel more alive."

Misty was still marveling at her parents, and pouring tea, when the alarm went off. All the girls screamed in chorus. She missed the cup she was holding and poured boiling hot tea on her left hand. She let go of the cup, and it rocketed to the floor where it smashed to smithereens on the slate floor.

Ignoring the searing pain in her hand, she set the pot down and ran into the foyer to see what had set the alarm to wailing like it was. "Stop that," she shouted at the flashing lights.

Hoodoo looked up at the panel and barked in protest. His addition to the noise only making matters worse.

Her mother was right behind her. "Punch in the code, sweetheart. Make it stop."

Her left hand red and blistering, Misty tried to remember the code. "I don't know the numbers." Tears rolled down her cheeks as she called for Angelique. "Where is the paper with the numbers on it, *ma chere*? I can't get this thing to shut off."

Before Angelique found the code, the police knocked on the door, and right behind them was Linc Castille looking handsome and sexy in his uniform.

Linc and the officers crowded into the foyer, and Linc did something technical and turned off the alarm. He cast a critical eye on her. "What happened? Why did the alarm go off?"

"Nothing happened. No one was in the foyer. The alarm went off all by itself."

"That doesn't happen. Not with one of my installations." Linc poked at the panel while the police officers verified that no one had broken into the house, and everything was in order.

The police left, and Misty introduced her mother. "Linc, this is my mother, Claire LeJeune."

"Nice to meet you, ma'am." Linc shook Claire's hand, and she cast a furtive glance at her daughter.

When Linc was done double-checking his handiwork, he left the house. Misty peeked through the front window and watched him drive away in his truck.

"He set the alarm off himself, Mystere. I read the deceit flowing through him when I took his hand."

"Why would he do that?"

"You tell me. I just met the man."

"Maybe he was angry that I canceled our date."

"Are you dating that young man?"

"I was thinking about it. Daddy said he was suitable for me. We cast a spell to draw my soulmate. He showed up."

"That man is not your soulmate, sweetheart. He wants something, Mystere. Something in this house."

Misty sighed. "It's the book. It's *always* the book. But why would Linc want the LeJeune Book of Shadows? He runs a business and is a security man."

"Perhaps that's not all he is."

After the crisis passed, Angelique made a burn poultice and bandaged it gently to Misty's blistering hand.

"That feels better already. Thank you."

Angelique patted her arm. "Would you like a glass

of wine, Madam? Your face is pale."

"Yes. Let's all have a glass of wine. I think we deserve it after being scared out of our wits for no reason."

Her mother narrowed her gaze. "Oh, there was a reason. That young man has an agenda. I'll figure out what it is."

Misty sighed. Why couldn't she meet another fantastic guy like Blaine? All she wanted was someone to love who could love her back for her, and not her family's magick.

The Apartment, New Orleans

Michele stood at the stove in their tiny apartment, boiling water for Kraft Dinner. "That was such an exciting day. Did you think there was something weird about Wannabe? Like the way he hopped up on the window sill and stared at Misty?"

Diana laughed. "Nope. He looked like a frog to me. A big, dumb, fat frog."

Michele got out the butter and the wieners. "Do you think Misty has powers strong enough to turn people into frogs?"

Charlotte pulled three bowls out of the sink-rack and laughed. "No. Nobody does anymore. That was back in the fairy tale days."

Diana giggled. "There were no fairy tale days, you guys. Those stories were never real."

Charlotte set the bowls down beside the stove and shrugged. "A lot of people think magick isn't real, but we know it is. We three were born to be witches."

"Maybe you were," said Diana, "I'm not sure about me."

Michele waved away her skepticism with her wooden spoon, brandishing it in the air like a wand. "Let's do a 'Charmed' marathon. I am so up for it."

Charlotte frowned. "We have to write our letters to Madam LeJeune first, telling her why we want to be witches. I might be up all night trying to find the right words."

"I've got mine done," said Diana.

Michele turned. "Finished? Already?"

Diana shrugged. "Yeah, what's the big deal. She only asked why you want to be a witch. How hard is that to put on a piece of paper?"

Michele wasn't sure. "I'll write down a few points after I'm done here. Then I can expand on them after the marathon."

CHAPTER SEVEN

Friday, January 6th.

<u>Nine Saint Gillian Street</u>

Misty's heart pounded in her chest when she heard footsteps on the third floor right above her head.

Who's up there? Is somebody looking for the book?

She jumped out of bed and almost trampled Hoodoo as she raced out of her room and down the wide hallway toward the narrow door that led to the third floor.

With the big Bernese hot on her heels, Misty raced up the stairs and almost smacked right into—*"Mother!* You scared me half to death. I thought there was an intruder up here."

"Intruder? You have an alarm, remember?"

"I don't think it's working properly, or it wouldn't have gone off by itself yesterday."

Her mother stared at her. "I told you. Linc made it go off remotely."

"But why would he?"

She laughed. "That's your mystery to solve, Mystere. He's your young man."

"No, he's not. We never even had a date. I don't trust him now." Misty focused on the besom in her mother's hand. "What are you doing up here?"

"I'm getting the classrooms ready."

"Classrooms?"

"If we're going to turn young girls into self-respecting witches, we need to do it properly, Mystere. There are many lessons needed to turn out a competent witch."

"We're holding classes? Like in a school?"

"That's the best way to teach students, don't you think?"

Misty hadn't given it much thought. "I guess so. Do I even have time to do this?"

"Actually, I do. The client who paid me to come had to change his plans. He canceled our sessions, so I'm free for the week. I figure, I can help you get started with the girls and set the foundation for you to have three young apprentices. The goddess touches our lives in mysterious ways, doesn't she?"

Yep. She sure did.

"And what if I don't want to give up my space," said a disgruntled voice from the corner of the empty room.

Misty searched the room, and her father revealed himself. "Is this where you hang out when you aren't in the kitchen, Daddy?"

"It's peaceful up here. A haven for me to sit and

think."

Her mother smiled over at her father's green glowy form. "And what could you possibly be thinking about, Josiah?"

"You are my every thought, Claire, and have been since the day we met."

"Flatterer."

Misty rolled her eyes. Well, at least they weren't fighting. "I'm going to let Hoo out and check the gardens. Mother, I'll set the girls on this task when they show up today."

"I'll make a list of the furniture we'll need, and you can order it on your internet."

Misty paused at the top of the steep staircase. "I haven't agreed to do this. Teaching is a lot of responsibility. What if I'm not ready? How do I know I'll be good at it?"

"You won't until you try, my sweet daughter. I have endless faith in you, and so does your father."

"Of course," her father said. "We know you can do it."

Her mother went back to sweeping. "We should test the girls first to see the extent of their natural abilities."

Her father nodded. "Yes. We must. An excellent idea."

"We'll set that as the first step going forward. There's no use wasting our time on no-talent youths with zero affinity for the life of a witch."

Misty frowned. "You make it sound like I'll teach

more than the three girls we already have."

Her mother swept the old broom through the attic. "Well, once we're set up, why not? No use wasting the space."

Misty retreated to the kitchen mumbling to herself. This was a terrible idea. Her parents were propelling her into something they wanted when they wouldn't even be there to help her see it through. It wouldn't be the first time.

The girls arrived after lunch. Misty ushered them inside and reset the alarm after hanging up their coats in the front closet.

"Come in girls," her mother said, calling them down to the kitchen. "We have exciting news for y'all."

Charlotte smiled as she sat down at the kitchen table and pulled a small notebook out of her purse. "What's the news, Madam Claire?"

"My daughter, the great and talented Misty, has decided to run a small school for budding, young witches, and you three will be tested as her first students."

Michele squealed, practically vibrating in her chair. "Ooo, thank you, Misty. Thankyouthankyouthankyou!"

Misty stood near the granite counter, still skeptical about the whole magick school idea. Her mother had embroiled her in crazy ideas before.

She winced as Angelique spread raw honey on her sore. Focusing on the healing skin, she recited a charm for the burn.

> *Aceso lend me your healing power*
> *Honey heal within the hour*
> *Pain and suffering set Mystere free*
> *Thankful are we for the fruit of the bee*
> *So mote it be*

Claire nodded to the girls and they joined in on the last line of the rejoinder. "So mote it be."

"I thank y'all," Misty said, covering the poultice with gauze. "I felt the energy. This burn will heal in no time, and we can all get back to work."

"In the meantime," her mother said, "why don't each of you girls read me your letters. Did y'all do your homework?"

"I'll go first." Charlotte pulled a folded piece of paper out of her purse and spread it out in front of her.

"Dear Madam LeJeune: I want to be a witch because I believe in magick. I believe in heightened intuition and psychic messages because I experience these phenomena from time to time. I have no experience, but am eager to learn and carry a strong belief that I was born to be a witch. Sincerely yours, Charlotte."

"Lovely, dear," said Claire. "Diana, let's hear yours."

Diana's face was a little flushed, but she unfolded her letter and offered a nervous smile.

"Dear Madam LeJeune: When I was nine years old,

my grandmother began teaching me to read tea leaves. As we went along, she told me she could see magickal power inside of me. I've never had the chance to do anything with it—if I do have it—which I truly want to. Yours truly, Diana."

"Excellent," said Claire. She pointed at Michele.

Michele sat straighter and nodded.

"*Dear Madam LeJeune: "I have spent hours of alone time trying to move objects with my mind, and I'm convinced I can do it. I need training. I'm reaching out for help because the only thing I want to be in life is a well-rounded witch. Sincerely, Michele.*"

Her mother nodded and pointed her way. "My Misty has that gift. I, myself, have never been able to master it. When she was a little girl, she used to float things over to her father, and he was so proud of her. Come on, girls. I'll show y'all where your training will be held once we have it furnished."

Misty waved them on ahead and took her time on the stairs. What had her mother gotten her into? By the time she climbed two flights of stairs, she was a little out of breath.

The girls were chattering and all talking at once. "Do we get to live here—like in a dorm?" asked Diana. "Or do we only come here in the daytime and go home at night like a regular school?"

"How much will tuition be?" asked Charlotte. "I've been saving, but I don't know if I have enough."

Her mother pressed an elegant finger to her lips.

"What would a fair price be for a semester of magick instruction?"

"They can't afford it," said Josiah from the corner of the room, but the only ones who heard him were Misty and her mother. "The knowledge Mystere will share is priceless."

Her mother threw out a number, and Misty shook her head. "No. We'll base the cost on what they can afford."

Her mother waved her words away. "Never mind. We'll work out the cost later. We have to get the classes running first. I'll need to go to the square to stock up on tools and materials we might need, and of course, I'll have to arrange some guest instructors."

Misty rolled her eyes. "I knew this would happen."

Angelique removed the essentials oils and other ingredients she needed from the antique step back cupboard and placed them in the center of the worktable. The recipe they were following was set in front of the girls, and they were each making a batch of the topical rub to combat colds and sore throats.

"How exciting is this? We're making this on our own." Michele washed her hands at the sink, turned to pick up a hand towel, and gave a little squeal. "Wannabe is on the window ledge again."

Angelique shook her head, walked to the window, and closed the curtains. "Begone, *monsieur la grenouille.*"

"He likes to see what we're doing," said Charlotte.

Misty made a face. "He's nosy. I think he'd be happier in the bayou with other frogs."

The protest arising from the girls at the table was interrupted by the doorbell and an enthusiastic round of barking from Hoodoo.

Her mother walked out with her. "I'll disengage the alarm, dear. We don't want a repeat of yesterday with your lying boyfriend arriving with a gaggle of uniforms."

"Not my boyfriend, Mother," said Misty as she continued to the door. When the red light flicked to green, Misty opened the door. "Lieutenant White, nice to see you. Come in."

She nodded to Ellis and yes, let him in too. "What brings the two of you to number nine Saint Gillian Street?" She motioned to the front parlor, and they followed her in and sat down on the sofa. "Would y'all care for tea or coffee?"

"No, thank you, Madam," said Lieutenant White. "Only a short visit. Fabian Landry's mother has filed a missing person's report, and she told us the last place her son was going before he disappeared was here to see you, Madam LeJeune. It seems he had it in his mind that you and he were becoming partners."

Misty made a face. "That's the story he told his mother?"

"She seemed to believe it, yes," said White. Detective Ellis hadn't said a word but seemed interested in the room décor.

"Mr. Landry came here yelling about working together," said Misty. "He was rude and aggressive—I'm not sure if he'd been drinking—he pushed Angelique, and knocked her to the ground. That was it for me. I told him to get out of my house, and thankfully, I haven't seen the man since."

"His mother said a driver brought his car home and dropped the keys in the mailbox."

Misty nodded. "True. Mr. Landry left his car on the street and never came back for it. I paid one of those drivers for hire to take it to his house. We only have one-hour parking out front on Saint Gillian, and I had no interest in him coming after me if he got a ticket."

"That was kind of you, Madam LeJeune," said Lieutenant White. "And after he left, you have no idea where he went?"

Misty shrugged and shook her head. "Where he went from here or why he didn't take his car, are questions I can't answer. I didn't see which way he went because I was helping poor Angelique up off the floor in the foyer at the time."

"Perhaps he left quickly thinking you would bring charges against him for assault."

"I should have, and still may. He hurt Angelique— her leg is bruised—and he broke my best crystal vase."

Lieutenant White got to his feet and offered Misty a card. "If you hear from him, will you let me know?"

Misty took the card and nodded. "Of course."

She opened the front door to see them out, and there

was Wannabe hopping on the front walk. The fat frog turned his head and focused big brown eyes on the cops.

Ribbet. Ribbet.

"That's one huge frog," Ellis said, shifting to the side of the walk. "Don't step on it, Lieutenant."

Misty retreated to the kitchen. "Mr. Wannabe is on the front walk, girls."

Diana jumped up. "Oh, no. He might hop into the road and get squished by a car."

Misty smiled. "That's what I was thinking."

After a five-minute break to rescue Wannabe from the front walk and relocate him near the fishpond, the girls were back to work with Angelique checking their progress every step of the way. "You make a great teacher, *ma chere*. Much better than I."

"Nonsense," her mother said. "You have the gift, Mystere. Teaching others will come naturally to you."

"Don't push her, Claire," said the voice from the corner of the room. "Perhaps our girl holds no desire to take on another commitment. Where will you be in a week's time? Not here helping her."

"Hold your tongue, Josiah. I'm speaking to our daughter."

Misty threw up her hands. "Both of you stop."

The girls grew wide-eyed, and Misty tried to explain. "My father—an incredibly powerful witch—died in this house, and still lives here. He talks to me, well . . . to us."

"You mean he's a ghost?" asked Charlotte.

"Uh-huh. Maybe y'all will get strong enough to speak to him one day."

"Ooh," said Diana. "That would be the coolest thing ever."

The doorbell rang, and Misty jumped. *I hope it's not the police again.*

"I'll get it," said Angelique, patting her on the shoulder as she passed by.

"And no, it isn't the police," her mother said.

"Stop doing that, or I'll stop thinking when you're around, Mother. I don't like you reading my mind."

Her mother chuckled. "I enjoy knowing what's going on under all that hair."

"You have beautiful hair, Misty," said Michele.

Angelique called out from the foyer. "Come help with de boxes, girls."

Misty gestured for them to do as Angelique asked. "I ordered more jars. They're here just in time."

The girls ran to help Angelique with the cases of jars, and Misty wondered what had happened to her peaceful existence. It was nice to have help now that her business had skyrocketed, but the chaos was a bit overwhelming.

She was taking a moment to catch her breath when her cell rang. "Ah, Linc the liar," she mumbled to herself while she debated the merits of talking to him. Reluctantly she pressed talk. "Hello?"

"Misty, I'm happy you took my call. Listen, I want to apologize for my abruptness the other day. I blamed you for setting off the alarm, when I think it was a glitch in the system. There is a lot of energy in your house."

"Thank you for your explanation. Apology accepted."

"I, uh, sense you're still annoyed with me. Maybe I could smooth things over when I take you out for that dinner?"

Yeah, right. "I'm sorry, Linc. That's not possible right now. My house is full of people, as you've seen, and I have no free time."

"That's too bad."

Isn't it?

Misty undressed in her room, and before crawling into bed, she checked the floor-safe to ensure the Book of Shadows was secure. She took it out of the protective bag, patted the worn leather cover, and then returned it to its safe place.

And then, just to be sure, she checked the alarm panel to ensure they were all locked up for the evening.

No need to be nervous. The alarm is on.

Footsteps. Misty jolted awake and jumped out of bed, sure she heard footsteps in the hallway. Hoodoo was asleep beside the bed and didn't bark. He always heard the smallest sound and recognized danger before she did.

Stop it. No one is in the house.

CHAPTER EIGHT

Saturday, January 7th.

<u>Nine Saint Gillian Street</u>

Hoodoo was in the back yard, and Misty stood on the back porch laughing as the big Bernese chased Wannabe around the fishpond. She glared at the cigarette between her fingers. She hadn't felt the urge to smoke for quite a while, but her nerves were on edge, and with good reason. Someone was after the Book of Shadows. She was sure of it, and after all, she was a psychic. She knew things.

First it was Landry. He made no secret about wanting it.

Now, Linc was acting weird, and she suspected he too was after her family secrets. But why would he want it? She needed a background check on Linc Castille. No. She needed a bodyguard—someone to watch the house, guard the book, and watch over her so she could get some goddamn work done.

Smoking and cursing. Perfect, she was turning into

Blaine.

She stepped off the deck and decided to spend some time in the herb garden to calm her nerves. When she'd picked a few fresh sprigs and cleared her head, she called Hoo and went inside. She gave him a biscuit from his jar in the mudroom, and he ran off into the sitting room to crunch it up and leave bits on the rug.

He did it every morning.

"You seem tired, Madam."

Misty washed her hands and set her cuttings beside the sink. "I haven't been sleeping well. The book is in jeopardy—I feel it."

Angelique, poured her a cup and set it before her.

Misty stirred in her milk and tinked the teaspoon on the side of her mug. "I must do more to protect it from thieves."

"I'm here, my child. I'll sound a warning."

She smiled over at her Daddy. "And what will I do, to defend myself against a big powerful man?"

"You have options, Mystere, and the power to do a great many things. Practice and preparedness are your watchwords."

"But I'm not prepared, and I should be. I'll take care of that starting today."

Angelique put a plate of bacon and scrambled eggs in front of Misty and sat down at the end of the table. "Eat, Madam. Your strength is declining."

"You're right, *ma chere*. I'm a mess."

Before she had time to swallow her last bite, Lieutenant White was on the phone. "We're on our way over to speak with you again, Madam. There is one point of our last discussion that needs clarification."

"I'll be here." Misty pressed *end* and let out a sigh. "The police are coming again. Perhaps I should turn Fabian back."

Angelique shook her head. "*Non*. Never. He is a bad man." She smiled. "Soon he will enjoy being *une grenouille*."

Misty wanted to believe that, but doubted it.

The doorbell rang, and Misty trudged her way into the foyer to open the door. "Good morning, gentlemen."

The two of them stared at her with suspicion written all over their sober faces. She pointed to the front parlor, and they trooped in and sat down like it was their second home.

"What do you wish to ask me?" Misty remained standing in the doorway.

Ellis took the lead, a gleam in his eye. "The forensic garage finished processing Mr. Landry's car, and your fingerprints were found on the passenger door, Madam. Could you give me an explanation?"

"Of course, I was in his car only once, and that was the night we first met—New Year's Eve."

Lieutenant White looked confused. "You've known Mr. Landry for less than a week?"

"I told you I barely knew the man, Lieutenant. And

yes, a week. My patience is wearing thin."

"I apologize, Madam. Finish your story."

"Thinking back on that night, I don't think it was a chance meeting at all. He joined me at the wine bar I am known to enjoy. He introduced himself and started talking to me. I think he'd been stalking me all along and knew my routine."

"But you'd never seen him before that night?" asked Ellis.

"No. Never." Misty paced in front of the hearth. "Near midnight, we danced one dance. When the evening ended, I went outside onto the street to look for a cab. Mr. Landry insisted on driving me home. At the time, I found it odd that he already knew where I lived."

Lieutenant White raised a dark eyebrow. "Did you ask him about it?"

"I did. He said everybody in town knew my family. You can verify my account by speaking to Jason, the maître d' at Vintage."

The two officers stood and made their way toward the door. Lieutenant White looked satisfied. Ellis looked like he might throw a fit.

"Thank you, Madam," White said, bowing his head. "That clarifies your fingerprints in his car. Sorry to bother you again."

Misty returned to the kitchen to finish her tea, and her mother joined her at the table.

"Are the students coming today?"

"I'm not sure. It's Saturday, Mother. With their part-time jobs, I think they work more on the weekends."

"What a shame they work. We were just getting started."

"I could use a break, Mother. In case you haven't noticed, I've been under a lot of stress."

Her father appeared in the corner of the kitchen. "Good morning to the beautiful women in my life."

Misty drew a deep breath and smiled. "Morning, Daddy."

"Ladies, on my way here, I noticed negative energy in the front parlor. There is a listening device of some sort in that room, and I haven't noticed it before as I made my rounds."

Misty stiffened. "What? Are you making that up, Daddy?"

"Negative, my child."

Misty grabbed her cell and pressed Lieutenant White's number. "Yes, Madam LeJeune, did you recall something you forgot to tell me?"

"No, but since y'all were here, there is a listening device in my front parlor. Whether it was you or your partner or a collaborative effort, I will bring charges down on your heads. You cannot invade my privacy like that, sir."

Adrenaline pumped through Misty's veins at an alarming rate, and sparks snapped from her fingertips.

"If there is a device in your parlor, Madam, I swear that was not placed there by me or by Detective Ellis. It must have come from some other source."

"Of course, you would deny it. I am, however, surprised you thought you could get away with it, knowing who and what I am, sir." Misty closed her eyes and said a few silent words wishing hell would rain down on the police station.

Ending the call, she took a couple of deep breaths and made her way back to the kitchen.

"I think, in my fury, I might have said that spell too quickly. Did I say hell or hail would rain down on them?"

Armed with a hot-temper, Misty retired to the sitting room and closed the door. She had to figure out what was going on. If it wasn't the cops who put the device in the front parlor, it had to be Linc. He had been in the house numerous times during the system installation and had every opportunity to hide one of those things.

Enough. She needed a bodyguard.

What about Luke Hyslop? She was fond of him—a little more than fond. As a native of New Orleans, they had a lot in common, and he understood who and what she was. Would he leave Blaine and come work for her? Even if Luke was willing, would Blaine let him go?"

She picked up her cell and called.

"Misty, are you okay, sweetheart?"

Hearing Blaine's voice still made her heart ache. "I'm having a little trouble with . . . this and that. I wondered if y'all could spare Lukey to come work for me, for a bit, or longer if he'd consider it?"

"Why do you need a bodyguard, Mist? Tell me the truth. What's going on?"

She told him about Fabian Landry stalking her and trying to get the book and then about Linc installing the system and acting weird, and about the police questioning her about Landry. She left out the part about turning Fabian into a frog. Blaine wasn't a big believer anyway.

"And this morning Daddy said there is a bug in the front parlor. I'm nervous, Beb."

"Someone planted a tag in your house? I don't like that, Mist. Not one bit."

"I don't know how to find it, and truthfully, I don't even know what I'm looking for."

There was a pause and then she heard Blaine light a smoke. "Give me a chance to sound Luke out on this. He seems pretty happy here compared to when he first arrived."

"I won't call him until you give me the green light."

"Appreciate it."

"Love you, Beb. For always."

"For always, Mist."

Misty emerged from the sitting room, and the girls were packaging orders on the worktable. She hadn't even heard the doorbell. "Hi, girls. I didn't hear y'all come in."

"We came for an hour before work," said Charlotte. "Did you see on the news where huge hail came down on the police station downtown and broke all the windows?"

Misty rubbed a hand over her face. "No, I didn't see it. We didn't get any hail here, did we Angelique?"

"*Non.*"

"That must have been right after Lieutenant White left here," her mother said. "How interesting."

Misty changed the subject and strode into the kitchen proper. "I never thought to ask you girls, but do your parents know you're coming here every day and hanging out with me?"

"We're adults, Misty," said Diana. "We don't live at home anymore."

"Y'all are very young adults. Do you live together?"

"We have an apartment above my grandmother's garage," said Diana. "It's small, but Gran makes us casseroles and cake."

"Cake is lovely, but nothing goes better with a cup of tea than a pan of warm brownies." Her mother cast a hopeful glance directly at Angelique.

"*Oui*, Madam. Let me make a batch."

Mother smiled, innocently. "Bless you, Angelique."

"Have you checked on Wannabe today, Diana?"

Diana eyes widened. "You knew I was just thinking about doing that, didn't you? You can read my thoughts."

Misty smiled. "Sometimes it happens."

"I so want to do that."

"Classes begin Monday morning, nine a.m.," Mother said.

Misty frowned at her. "The furniture isn't ordered yet."

"Or so you think, daughter. The store promised we'd have it for today."

Diana squealed. "Ooo, I can't wait to see what our school will look like."

Her mother pointed to a pad and pen on the table. "Let's make a list of supplies we'll need to start. Monday, we'll take a trip to the square and buy what we need."

Charlotte pointed to her bare arms and giggled. "Look, I've got goosebumps. This is like a dream coming true while I'm awake."

Misty couldn't help but get swept up with them. The girls were so cute and enthusiastic. Having them around was the highlight of her day. Maybe this was one of her mother's better ideas, after all.

After dinner, Misty settled in the sitting room with a book while her mother and Angelique worked on the classroom upstairs. The furniture had arrived, and after an hour of the delivery men loudly cursing the narrow staircase, the tables, chairs, and storage cupboards had been lugged up to the third floor.

Misty's cell rang on the coffee table in front of her,

SCHOOL FOR RELUCTANT WITCHES · 107

and she checked the screen to make sure it wasn't Linc Castille. She didn't recognize the number. With hesitation, she accepted the call. "Hello?"

"Misty, it's Luke Hyslop. Blacky talked to me about your situation, and I'd be glad to come back and check it out." Luke spoke very slowly—his Louisiana drawl similar to her own.

"Thank you so much, Luke. I wasn't sure you'd be open to leaving the Agency or coming home, for that matter."

"I do love working with Blaine, but I also miss my home. I'll enjoy spending time with y'all."

"When are you coming? I'll pick you up at the airport."

"Eleven tomorrow morning."

"Can't wait to see you," said Misty. And she meant it. Luke was one of her favorite people.

CHAPTER NINE

Sunday, January 8th.

A heightened sense of anticipation had Misty out of bed before six and showered and dressed by seven. She and Angelique did a quick clean up and tidying of the main floor, and then Misty spent half an hour getting the room next to hers ready for Luke Hyslop. It would be so nice to have him around.

Quiet and intelligent and so sensitive, he was a man with a broken heart, who moved away from Louisiana after a terrible car accident took the lives of his wife and baby daughter. There was a long healing process after a tragedy of that magnitude and Luke was far from being over it.

Misty placed an orange candle she'd cleansed and consecrated on the dresser in the room she was preparing for Luke. She lit the candle and said a few encouraging words.

The time has passed
This spell I cast

From east to west you roam
Your heart has bled
For the one, you wed
Let peace welcome you home
So mote it be

Louis Armstrong Airport, New Orleans

Misty waited in the arrival's lounge watching the passengers from Austin, Texas, come through the arrivals gate. Luke didn't see her at first as he emerged in a flood of traffic, but Misty spotted him right off. He looked good. He'd put on a bit of weight, and his long auburn hair was tied neatly back with a blue bandana. She'd almost forgotten how tall and good looking he was. Almost.

He saw her, gave a little wave, and hurried towards her carrying his one piece of luggage. He set the bag down and pulled her into an awkward side hug. "I'm glad you need me, Misty. I was getting a bit homesick in Austin."

She stepped back and patted his arm. "Then I'll make you some Cajun comfort food tonight to welcome you home."

Luke took things in stride as Misty parked at the back of her house and opened the garden gate for him to pass through. He stood by the fishpond, gazing up at the old mansion. His memory flooded with images from the last time he'd been here. They'd been searching for Misty and found her unconscious and held prisoner in a dark secret room in her own home.

Number nine Saint Gillian was formidable. He had no idea how many secrets would be locked up in a place like this, but he knew enough to respect them.

A cool shiver ran the length of his spine as he took a step forward, and a fat frog hopped in front of him. He caught himself from tripping on the thing and shuffled off to the side. "Whoa, froggy. Watch where you're going."

Misty giggled and pushed the fatso off the walk. "That's Wannabe. He lives here in the yard."

"What does he wannabe?" asked Luke, catching a funny vibe from the thing. "A handsome prince?"

"I guess maybe he did," said Misty. "Not now."

As they entered the back door, Luke glanced at the new locks he knew Blaine installed. It would take him a few days to check out the security system and verify its validity. Blaine told him Misty didn't trust the man who'd done the installation.

Luke set his bag down in the hallway and followed Misty into the kitchen. "Luke, I'd like you to meet Angelique, my assistant, and very dear friend."

And Hoodoo practitioner. He knew her by reputation from growing up in the bayou. "It's a pleasure, Madam."

Luke shook the big Cajun lady's hand and felt her energy tingle against his palm. Good gracious, this was a house filled with magickal power.

Angelique released his hand with a smile and

slipped back behind the kitchen counter. "I fixed lunch, Madam."

"Thank you. Where's Mother?"

The Cajun woman pointed off toward the back of the house. "Up in de classroom fussing."

Misty nodded. "Sit down, Luke. After we eat, we can get you settled."

Claire LeJeune floated into the room a few moments later, and the energy shifted. Luke had always been attuned to the presence of magick. He'd been raised by his grandmother who—like Angelique—was well known in the Hoodoo world.

Misty gestured to the raven-haired beauty and smiled. "This is my mother, Claire. Mother, this is Luke Hyslop. He's come home from Austin to watch over us."

Claire held her hand out to him. "Welcome. Misty's last two prospective suitors were both liars and thieves, Mr. Hyslop. I don't believe the second is finished with her yet."

Luke smiled. "That's why I'm here, Madam. To protect y'all from men like that. I know there are a great many who covet your family's book and the power y'all wield."

Claire rolled her eyes, and Misty laughed. "Daddy, you're so silly." Misty looked to him and smiled. "Daddy said he should have taken the book with him when he died. Then none of this would be happening."

Huh, Blaine warned him to have an open mind about the magick of the LeJeune family tree. He looked to the corner Misty indicated and nodded his head. "Wish I could hear you, sir. I always wanted to meet *Monsieur LeJeune* when you were alive, and so did my grandmother. It's an honor to be in your home."

***

After lunch, Misty showed Luke to his room on the second floor. It wasn't anything overdone, just a big comfy bed, an antique dresser, and a desk and lamp for him to set up how he liked. "I put you right next door to me and the book. I'll show you where I keep it as soon as you're settled in here.

Luke glanced at the orange candle on the dresser and nodded. "It smells fantastic in this room. Are you trying to spellcast me, Misty?"

"I wanted you to feel at home. It was a simple cleansing, to make you feel welcome."

His expression softened. "I do, and I thank you for that. We've always been kind of on the same page. The way we were raised and our beliefs and whatnot. It's time I get back to that, to who I was."

Misty's heart ached for him. "That's essentially the reason I had to come home too. In Austin, as much as I loved Blaine, I always felt out of place. It was never my home."

Luke left his bag on the bed to unpack later. "Show me where you keep the book."

Misty led Luke next door to her room. She pulled up the rug that covered the hinged section of hardwood, pressed the catch, and the lid opened to reveal the safe concealed below. "There it is. Do you think that's safe enough?"

"And only you know the combination?" he asked.

"Yes."

"Let me think about it. Show me where you think the tag is, and I'll see if I can find it. I brought a bug detector with me in case it's not easy to locate."

"Daddy said the negative energy was coming from the front parlor. There may be nothing to it."

They descended the wooden staircase together, and Luke stopped at the door of the parlor. He gave her arm a gentle squeeze. "Give me a few minutes."

Misty left Luke searching the parlor and was on her way to the kitchen when Blaine called. "Hey, Mist. Did Luke arrive?"

"He did, and thanks, Beb, for letting him come home. I feel safer already."

"Did he find the tag?"

"He's looking for it now. I can have him call you."

"Do that. And yeah, when I asked him if he'd consider your offer, he seemed pleased—relieved, I think. He misses New Orleans."

"He said he was a little homesick, but also how much he loved working with y'all."

"Call me with anything."

"Thanks, Beb."

He sounds happy. I should try to be happy too.

Luke caught up with her in the kitchen, and he had the tiny thing in his hand. "I found it. Give me your best guess on who put it there."

"The person with the best opportunity would be Linc Castille, who installed the new system. The last people in the room before Daddy noticed it, were two police officers here on another matter."

"I'll take a quick look at the panel, and then I'll set up my laptop upstairs and see what I can find on Linc Castille."

"You don't have to start work right away. Tomorrow will be soon enough."

Luke grinned. "What would I do if I wasn't working?"

"I can think of a few things. The first being, enjoying a beer on the back porch with me while soaking in the sense of being home."

Luke nodded. "I can definitely do that."

After their beer together in the crisp January air, Misty entered the house through the back door. Luke waited for Hoodoo to catch up and locked the door behind them. They were exiting the mudroom when the doorbell rang.

"It's Sunday. I'm not working today, Angelique. Tell them to make an appointment." Misty went into the kitchen to take a bottle of wine from the cooler for dinner, and Angelique went to the front door.

She returned and spoke in a whisper, "Madam, Mrs. Landy wishes to speak to you."

Misty cursed and set down her wine. "I don't want to talk to Mrs. Landry."

"Landry. That's the man who was stalking you."

"Yes. It must be his mother or his wife—if he had one."

"I'll go with you." Luke nodded for her to take the lead and they trudged down the hall together. When she stopped in the foyer, Luke slid in beside her. The warm energy emanating from Luke's body flowed into hers.

It felt wonderful and reassuring.

"Mrs. Landry?" she said, to a short, gray-haired woman wearing glasses and an angry expression.

"Madam LeJeune, you know where my son is, and I demand you tell me. The police are convinced you don't know, but I know better. He was determined to speak with you, and my Fabian would not have changed his mind. He is an extremely focused boy. He was a psychic, and every bit as gifted as you."

"I'm sure he was, but I can't help you. He's gone, and I don't think we'll be seeing him anytime soon."

"Where did he go when he left this house?"

"As I recounted to the officers who came here, Fabian pushed into my home and knocked Angelique to the floor. We had words, and suddenly he was gone. That's all I can tell you."

"You're lying."

Misty reached into her pocket and gripped her wand.

Lying, flying

From your mind, these thoughts go
Forget what it is you think you know

Mrs. Landry's face took on a blank look and then, she blinked and smiled. "It's been lovely speaking with you, Madam. I'd better be getting back home to see if Fabian called. Have a nice day."

Angelique closed the door and locked it.

Luke looked Misty in the eye. "Should I ask what you did to her?"

"I made her slightly forgetful of her suspicions."

"And do you know where Fabian is?"

"He actually doesn't go by Fabian anymore."

Luke raised an eyebrow. "He took a new identity?"

Misty nodded. "Mr. Wannabe."

Luke blinked and then doubled over laughing. "Oh, shit. I think I need another beer."

CHAPTER TEN

Monday, January 9th.

<u>Nine Saint Gillian Street</u>

Misty slept soundly. The first good night's rest she'd had since New Year's. Her subconscious mind relaxed by the presence of Luke Hyslop sleeping in the next room. She got out of bed and shrugged on a terry robe feeling positive energy surrounding her. Hoodoo was already standing at the door to the hallway wagging his tail. "Come on, boy. I'll let you outside."

When Misty reached the back door, she saw Luke in the yard smoking and staring at the fishpond. Dressed in snug jeans and a Saint's sweatshirt, his long auburn hair hung loose on his shoulders. He took her breath away.

Barefoot, she ventured across the dew-soaked grass and stood next to him.

"Cool morning," he said, staring across the little pond into the greenery. "I was looking for your frog and didn't see him."

"Angelique wants to take him to the bayou. She

doesn't like him hopping around the yard."

"That's a good idea. We should do that."

Misty nodded and rubbed her arms. "Okay, we will."

He looked down and frowned. "We should go in. It's too cold for you to be out here in bare feet."

She shivered, and he ran his palms up and down her arms. "Come on. Let's get you inside and get you warmed up."

Misty chuckled. "You're here to defend me from robbers and unscrupulous men, not from catching a cold."

He pressed his hand to the small of her back as they walked, the heat from his touch radiating up her back. "What can I say, I'm a dedicated man. I won't let anything get you. Not even a cold."

For the first day of magick school, the girls arrived at ten to nine. Excited and talking en masse, Misty waited for them to quiet down so she could introduce Luke.

"This is Luke Hyslop, girls. He'll be staying here with us and keeping us safe. Luke, this is Charlotte, Michele, and Diana, my students—actually Mother's students—since she decided to teach them."

Luke dipped his chin and gave them each a kind smile. "Morning, girls. Nice to meet y'all. You look excited to learn what Madam LeJeune has in store to teach today, and well, you should be. I know I would be."

Diana nodded, her ebony pixie cut bouncing in every direction. "I've never been more anxious to go to school in my entire life. I used to hate school, and now I can't wait to start. I couldn't sleep all night, thinking about it."

Misty smiled as they tore up the stairs to the third-floor classroom. When the clamor died down, she chuckled. "I wish I had half their energy and enthusiasm."

Luke chuckled. "I'll do some research on Linc Castille. I'll be at the desk in my room if you want me."

Misty did want him, but that wasn't what he meant. "Did you get a chance to check the alarm panel?"

"I did, and it seems to be working. The only concern I had was the code and whether Linc might have a way to bypass that part of the system. Until we're in the clear, I think it should be changed every morning."

Misty nodded. "Whatever you think is best. I trust your judgment."

On the third floor, things were happening. The three girls sat on the far side of a medium-size worktable, and Claire stood on the opposite side facing them.

"We have to begin by testing for your natural abilities. These are three old wands that used to belong to my late husband, and y'all can use them until you create your own."

The girls picked up the wands handling them gently like they were sticks of dynamite.

"Who knows the purpose of a wand?" asked Claire.

"To turn men from frogs into princes," Charlotte joked.

Claire laughed. "While that may be the end result, once in a long while, no. A wand directs a witch's energy and will."

"Could you point with your finger, if you needed to?" Diana asked.

"Yes, a seasoned witch could, but a wand is more accurate and focused." Claire picked up her wand and held it up for them to see. "Each of you, collect a wand in your dominant hand and imagine the energy from your body channeling down your arm, through your hand, and extending in a powerful stream through your fingers."

Charlotte picked one up, closed her eyes, and pointed.

Bam.

A jolt shot across the room, and the hundred-year-old wallpaper caught on fire with a loud *pouff.*

The girls screamed, but Claire was there, blotting the fire out with a besom. With the wall extinguished, she turned and smiled. "Very impressive, Charlotte. Now, who's next?"

Misty ran up the stairs when she heard the screaming. The scent of char tainted the air, and there was a thin wisp of smoke dancing along the ceiling. "My, my, what's happening up here with you, young witches?"

"Nothing," said Claire, shifting to stand in front of a

large scorched patch on the wall behind her. "I'm testing the girls with your father's old wands."

"Well, if you've already started a fire, that's a good sign. Who's turn is it next?"

"I'll go next," Michele said, sitting up straighter. She held the wand out in front of her, closed her eyes, and screwed up her face. Nothing happened. Her excitement fell. "I didn't feel anything."

Misty waved away her concern. "Don't be discouraged. It takes time to train your energy. This is your first day. Maybe you're nervous. Maybe the wand doesn't suit you. It's nothing to worry about."

"But it was Charlotte's first day too," said Diana, "and she lit the wall on fire."

Misty eyed the damage, and her mother gave an innocent shrug. "Not to worry. It's time that old wallpaper came off anyway. I'll have someone come and remove it, and we'll fit new shelving all across that wall for all our supplies."

Claire nodded her approval.

Misty brought the girls back to their testing. "Go ahead, Diana. I want to see you take your turn before I go downstairs."

Diana nervously picked up the wand in front of her, closed her eyes, and held her arm straight out in front of her. Nothing happened for a few seconds, and then a few sparks trickled out the end of the wand.

Clair gave her wand a flick, and confetti rained down over the three of them. "Congratulations, girls.

With hard work, you each will be working witches by the end of the first semester."

They squealed, and Misty retreated downstairs. She wasn't sure who was having more fun, the girls or her mother.

Misty descended the stairs as Angelique greeted her first client of the week and invited her in. Even from the distance from the stairs to the foyer, Misty felt deceit and betrayal oozing from the pores of the well-fashioned brunette. Angelique gathered her luxurious fur and turned to hang it in the closet.

"Madam LeJeune, hello," she said, offering her a dazzling smile. "How lovely to meet you, I'm Suzanne Bordelon." She offered her hand, and Misty accepted it to assess if the negative energy was directed toward her specifically, or cloying around her and directed at someone else.

The sensation of spiders scuttling up her arms made contact quick and uncomfortable. "You wish to have a Tarot reading, Miss Bordelon?"

"I do. Please call me Suzanne. May I call you, Mystere?"

"No, thank you. Madam LeJeune will be fine."

The smile vanished as Suzanne Bordelon followed Misty into the newly cleansed front parlor. After Luke removed the listening device, Angelique wrought a cleansing spell on the room to free it from negative energy. Several cinnamon-scented candles burned for further protection.

"Tea, Madam?" asked Angelique.

Misty read the concern on her assistant's face and knew that she too could sense this woman's true nature. "Tea would be wonderful, but first, would you ask Luke to join us. I believe he's in his room."

"*Oui*, Madam."

Luke had his laptop up and several internet searches running when Angelique appeared at his door. The woman seemed flushed in the cheeks and winded as if she'd taken the stairs at too quick a pace. "Is something wrong, Madam LaFontaine?"

"*Oui*, de new client is a danger to Madam. She wishes you near her."

Luke hopped up and followed Angelique downstairs. He met Misty's gaze as he entered the front parlor. She dipped her head and went back to her reading. He took his cue, picked up a book on divination, and settled in the chair by the window.

Misty gave the woman her Tarot reading—a Celtic cross spread—and the client seemed attentive enough, nodding the odd time to agree with what Misty said.

Angelique had just come in to serve tea when the client said, "Madam LeJeune, I have it on good authority that you recently aided the police in finding Ryan Cormier. I'd like to do a story on you and your incredible abilities."

Misty didn't seem surprised. "And who told you

that, Miss Bordelon?"

The brunette shrugged. "I'm a professional, Madam. I never reveal my sources."

"And I am a professional as well. I never give interviews." Misty stood and gestured toward the door. "You came here under false pretenses, Miss Bordelon. I'll have to ask you to settle up with Angelique and then leave."

The woman made no move to stand or do as Misty asked. Luke stood and strode over to the parlor table. "Madam LaFontaine, would you please retrieve Miss Bordelon's coat? She'll be leaving now."

The reporter turned and gave Luke the stink-eye. "And who are you, her bodyguard?"

Luke smiled. "Exactly."

Without further fuss, he escorted the woman to the foyer, ensured she settled up what she owed, and showed her out. When she stepped outside, he locked the door and changed the code on the panel. He jotted the numbers in his notebook and slipped it into his shirt pocket.

Misty sat at the table in the parlor, putting the cards back into the velvet bag that held them. "Detective Ellis told her. He was the only one who could've done it."

She opened her cell, made a call, and put it on speaker so he could hear."

"Madam LeJeune," the man on the other end said. "I didn't expect to hear from you so soon—considering our last call. I hope you know how troubled I am over that misunderstanding."

Misty frowned. "Lieutenant White, a reporter came into my home asking me about Ryan Cormier and the part I played in his recovery. She said someone told her about me and that *someone* could only have been you or Detective Ellis. My money is on Ellis."

"Apologies, Madam. I assure you I know nothing of this. I'm sure Ellis told no one as you requested, but I'll verify it."

Misty sighed. "I've tried to help the police in the past, Lieutenant, but publicity puts me in an awkward position. It also makes me question whether or not I can trust you."

"Madam, I assure you I will look into this. I am truly sorry this happened. Moreso, because I have another case, I hoped to ask you to consult on."

Misty shook her head. "I don't know if that's a good idea, given the situation."

"Please, Madam. Let us not punish the innocent for the actions of a few meddlesome people.

Misty deliberated for a moment and then rolled her eyes. "Fine. Email the file to my bodyguard. I'll have him give you his contact information."

"I'm sorry, Madam. Police files can't be sent to civilians."

Misty looked up at him and smiled. "Luke Hyslop is a Texas Ranger, sir. A highly qualified officer in his own right."

"Very well. I'll take his information. If he checks

out, we can handle it your way. And I assure you *no one* will find out you are assisting me."

Misty took the call off speaker and handed him her cell. Luke gave Lieutenant White his particulars, then said, "Yes, sir. I understand. Once I receive the information, I'll read through it and decide if we can help. Yes, sir, as quickly as I can." He pressed end and smiled. "We have more work to do."

Misty frowned and let out a long sigh. "I don't trust them. Ellis is a non-believer and a treachery."

Luke shrugged. "Perhaps he needs help with his behavior like Mr. Wannabe."

Misty burst out laughing. Not only was he glad to see a smile on her face, he was glad he put it there. Misty was the kind of woman who deserved to smile.

Claire descended the staircase from the third floor with three stampeding girls galloping behind her. They headed straight to the foyer in a whirl of energy and excitement. "Misty, love," she called to the main floor. "We're going on an outing to the square to introduce the girls to some of the practitioners and to pick up supplies we need."

Misty popped out of the parlor and hustled to join them. "I'm coming too. I need to get out of the house for a while, and so does Luke."

"We can't all fit in your car, Misty. If you come, that means we'll have to take the bus."

Misty shook her head. "I'll call a cab and ask for a

seven-passenger vehicle."

"Or a yellow school bus," Luke said, shrugging into his leather jacket.

Misty chuckled and accepted her coat from Charlotte. "Tomorrow, Luke will trade in the Honda and we'll get ourselves a yellow school bus."

Luke barked a laugh. "I was kidding."

Misty winked. "So was I. How about, we'll get something bigger than my Honda. We all have to get to the bayou to collect roots soon. We might as well be prepared."

She looked at him. "From bodyguard to police consultant to car dealer and on only the first day."

Luke chuckled. "A many-faceted job. I like that."

Jackson Square, French Quarter

Jackson Square was teeming with visitors when they arrived. A must-see destination in the French Quarter that offered artists, musicians, performers as well as fortune tellers, palm readers, psychics, Tarot readers and vendors with stalls chock full of specialty items.

Her mother corralled the girls like a goose with goslings. "Don't get lost now. Let's stay together."

Luke took hold of Misty's elbow and checked with her that she didn't mind. "I don't want to lose you in this crowd."

They walked around the plethora of tents and booths, and Misty stopped and chatted with many of the people she knew. She noticed how Luke kept a close watch on the passersby and generally steered her away from crowded areas.

She also noticed how his assessing gazes seemed to linger on her. There was no complaint on her side, though perhaps he was just a thorough bodyguard. Ha, that made her wonder how thorough he might be in the future.

When he was looking particularly serious, she stepped up close to him and tilted her mouth to whisper in his ear. "What has you looking so serious? Is someone following me?"

He set his hands on her hips, but he didn't move away. "Nope. Nobody. Just assessing the situation. All good."

She winked at him, and they moved on. "Yep. All good."

Her mother found them about an hour later. She and the girls were laden down with bags, and Luke helped carry the load across the street to one of the cafés.

Diana plunked onto the bench of the booth and scooted over to let Charlotte in. "I'm so tired, but that was so much fun. Once I'm trained, maybe I'll rent a stand here in the square to read tea leaves."

Her mother dismissed that idea. "Young lady, you have the privilege of being trained by the LeJeunes. You'll accomplish more than a tea reading stand by the time we get through with you."

Misty ordered a glass of Merlot, and Luke ordered Miller. "Are you hungry?" she asked him.

"Always," he said.

Yes, she was sure it took a lot of calories to fuel a man as big and muscled as he. "If I order a po'boy, will you split it with me? I can never finish one myself."

Luke nodded. "Perfect. Whatever you choose is fine by me. I eat anything put in front of me."

The oversized cab pulled up to the curb in front of nine Saint Gillian Street, and Luke sensed something was off. "Stay in the cab, ladies. I want a chance to check out the house." He jumped out, jogged up the flagstone walk, and tried the front door. It was locked as it should have been, but the hair on the back of his neck stood on end and prickling him.

Someone was here.

Luke used his key, went inside, and examined the panel. Everything seemed to be in order, and yet, something wasn't right. It took him ten minutes to clear the three floors of the house. When he was certain there was no intruder inside, he beckoned to Misty, and she brought the girls in.

"Did you check?" Misty asked as they stepped inside the foyer.

Luke knew she meant the book, and he shook his head. "From what I could see, nothing was touched. You go check."

She returned to the top of the staircase moments later and called down to him. "All good."

Claire sat in the front parlor, closed her eyes, and concentrated. The girls gathered around her and watched with interest. After several minutes, she opened her eyes. "He was here."

"Who, Mother?"

"Linc Castille searched the house but found nothing."

"I don't understand why he wants it."

Luke frowned. "That's because we don't know enough about him. I'll figure him out. I'll work on it now."

Misty nodded. "While you do that, Mother and I will cast a ward around the property. This is getting nerve-racking"

Claire gave Michele her coat and headed straight into the kitchen. Misty's cupboards were well-stocked and she searched until she found what she was looking for in a huge container on the bottom shelf. "Here they are, castor beans."

"Castor beans?" Misty said. "I was thinking more along the lines of salt combined with something poisonous, like Lily of the Valley."

"Nonsense, sweetheart. We'll go with the beans. They've always worked for me. Tried and true."

"I'm with Misty on this," Josiah said from the corner. "I'm leaning towards the Lily of the Valley. It's one of my favorites for protection."

"Oh, sweetheart, you never wanted to try anything new. Though, I loved you all the same."

"Thank you, darling."

She gave her belated love a smile and gathered her pupils. "Let's go, girls. We need a sprinkling of beans all around the foundation of the house."

Once the beans were in place, Misty, Angelique, Claire, Luke, and the three girls joined hands in the back yard and raised their eyes upward while Misty invoked the spell.

> *Goddess of the moon*
> *Hear my call*
> *Protect my house*
> *From wall to wall*
> *Surround number nine with goodness and light*
> *Help me in my hour of fright*
> *So mote it be.*

Misty repeated her chant three times and felt calmness descend on her. "It's working already."

Luke smiled. "Good. Less for me to worry about."

Misty said goodnight to her mother and Angelique when they turned in and went upstairs to their rooms. Her mother had always read in the evenings, and Angelique used her free time to make jewelry from crystals. Luke was about to leave as well to work on his research when he turned back. "Are you heading up to bed too?"

Misty shook her head. "I don't think I could sleep if I tried. I might have a drink and maybe watch a movie."

"Do you want some company?"

Misty chuckled. "You might be forced to watch a chick flick."

Luke chuckled. "I might not stay for the whole movie. I need to read the police file, Lieutenant White sent over, but one beer won't hurt."

Misty took that as her cue to grab them a couple of bottles of beer and pop some popcorn. When they were set, they headed into the sitting room. She settled on the sofa with the controllers, and Luke took the chair. She passed him his drink and then found a movie she liked on Netflix.

"You'll love this one."

He took a long haul on his beer and chuckled. "You sure?"

Misty pushed at him with her socked foot, and he laughed. He returned the favor by squeezing her toes and making her laugh. "Pretty sure."

The Apartment, New Orleans

"Could you believe we cast a protection spell today?" Charlotte pulled her dark hair back and changed into her uniform for an eight o'clock shift. "I'll be so glad when we don't have to work at a regular job anymore."

"There's not much money in being a witch," said Michele. "That's probably why Misty has to sell her healing products."

"I wonder when we'll be able to start giving readings," said Charlotte, shuffling the new deck of Tarot cards she'd chosen at Jackson Square earlier in the day. "That would bring in some cash to help pay the rent."

"I think we need to learn a whole lot more before we're ready," said Diana. "A whole lot."

CHAPTER ELEVEN

Tuesday, January 10th.

<u>Nine Saint Gillian Street</u>

Luke rose early, had a quick smoke in the back yard, then returned to his room to finish reading the file Lieutenant White sent to him. He'd planned to have one beer with Misty and head up to his room to read through the reports last night, but it just hadn't happened. He liked watching her while she watched the movie. He liked spending any time with her. It was the first time he'd held any interest in a woman since his wife died. It was a new development and, if he was honest with himself, a welcome one.

She was talented, independent, and yes, he'd noticed how beautiful she was too. He tried to push any inappropriate thoughts about Misty out of his mind and concentrate on the words on the screen in front of him.

So far, there had been three linked murders in the city. All three bodies were well-dressed, men in their early thirties found close to the Mississippi. Three different areas, but each of them poisoned by an unknown substance.

Poison was generally a woman's weapon.

His door was open, and Misty filled the opening, holding a cup of coffee in each hand. "You're up early."

"Couldn't sleep," said Luke, accepting the coffee with his thanks. "A lot is going on in my life suddenly."

Misty stepped behind him to read his screen. Her hand rested casually on his shoulder, and a shiver ran down his spine.

"These men were poisoned?"

He swallowed and tried to focus. "The medical examiner for each corpse said they each ingested something."

"They're sure they ingested the poison?"

"There were no needle marks found."

"That doesn't mean there wasn't any. Injection points are almost impossible to detect in some cases."

Luke picked up his coffee and took a sip. "How do you feel about the case? Do you think you could help?"

"In order to help, I'd have to go to each victim's house and spend a little time. That would have to be arranged to keep it private. I'm not having another reporter following me around asking questions."

"If you want me to talk to Lieutenant White, I can get the first visit set up for you. You don't have to help them, though. You don't owe them anything, especially after exposing your involvement in your last case."

"I'll go, but make it clear that it's you, White, and me. No Ellis. I don't trust him."

"Copy that, boss."

Misty giggled and ruffled his auburn hair. "Let's go downstairs and get some breakfast. I'm starving."

Luke agreed, getting out of his room was likely a good idea. It had been too long since he'd been attracted to a woman, let alone wondered about kissing one. He might make a fool of himself if they didn't get somewhere safer.

Misty helped Angelique clean up the kitchen after breakfast. They had to work on more orders that had come in on the internet overnight. Her mother would have to handle the girls alone for the morning and start them on their next lesson. Funny, since she'd gotten her whole witch school idea, her mother hadn't mentioned a word about going back to Lily Dale.

I hope she's back to stay.

With the recipe for the love potion on the table, Misty took the ingredients they needed out of the cupboard. Her cell rang in the pocket of her black work apron, and she checked to see who it was. Blaine.

"Hey, Beb. What's up?"

"Just checking in to see how Luke is working out."

"Very well. He's working on a case the police want me to help with."

"He's thorough. You can trust him."

"I do. I had another thought, Beb. I told you about

the classes Mother and I are starting, didn't I?"

"Umm . . . you may have mentioned it, but I'm not sure."

"Well, Mother's in town, and we've taken on three young girls who want to learn about magick and what we do. We've transformed the third floor into a makeshift magick school. I was wondering—and I'm leaving this totally up to you—but I thought Casey might like to join. He's always been inquisitive about Tarot and keen to learn what I know. He could stay with me for a while. It would be fun to have him."

"True. He has. I'll ask him if he's interested. Hang on."

Misty held the line, and Blaine returned a couple of minutes later, laughing. "He's more than enthused, Mist, he's losing it, he's so excited. He wants to come right away."

"The sooner, the better."

"Okay, I'll call back when I find him a flight."

"I'm glad, Beb. You know how much I love him. Tell him he's only missed two days, and he can catch up."

"Any other boys in the class?" asked Blaine.

"Nope. All girls. One about eighteen and the others a couple of years older."

Blaine chuckled. "Older women. He'll be pumped."

Hoodoo ran to the front door barking, and Misty came out to see what all the excitement was. Luke was bent, peering through the sidelight, giving her a glorious view of his backside in tight black jeans. "There's a man coming through the gate, Misty. Do you recognize him?"

Misty crowded in beside Luke and peeked out the window. "Yes, that's Detective Ellis, the purveyor of treachery."

Luke eyed him up and looked like he was about to go out and shoo him away when Ellis tripped over something invisible and crashed to the ground. Rolling to grab his ankle, he cursed and made an agonized face. "Help. I think my foot is broken."

Misty shrugged and turned back to the kitchen. "Well, at least we know the ward is working properly. Should we leave him there as a warning to other ne'er-do-wells?"

"You're kidding, right?" Luke chuckled, and then sobered when he realized she wasn't. "No. I'll take care of it. I'll call an ambulance and send him on his way."

Luke opened the door and stepped outside.

The girls ran down from the third floor to see what was happening, and Misty pointed. "Don't go out. You can see through the window. Detective Ellis betrayed my trust, and the protection spell is working. He fell and broke his ankle before he could get to us."

"That's so amazing," said Charlotte. "Will you let us write down that spell, Misty? I'm getting castor beans to put around Diana's Gran's house. I want her to be safe when we're at work and over here."

"That sounds like a wonderful idea. And, speaking

of wonderful news, a young friend of mine from Austin has a special interest in magick. I've invited him to join the school. He's flying here from Texas to stay with me."

"Ooh," said Diana, "is he good looking?"

"Is grass green?" asked Misty with a wink.

The girls squealed all the way back to the classroom, and Misty giggled to herself. "Wait until they meet Casey. Mother will meet her match."

Sirens sounded as the ambulance turned the corner of Saint Gillian Street. The paramedics walked up to the steps with a stretcher, loaded up Detective Ellis, and took him away.

Luke came in, wearing a smile. "He won't be around for a while."

"Karma bit him in the ass," said Misty.

"I think the LeJeunes helped Karma bite him in the ass."

Misty giggled. "I love it when a spell comes together. Now I need a good one for Linc Castille. He'll be back, and I don't know enough about him to know if a protection spell will keep him away from my book."

Luke frowned. "I'm sorry. I haven't had a lot of time to delve into his background."

She waved away his concerns. "We've been busy. Now, let's go trade in the Honda and grab some lunch."

Luke swept a hand toward the door. "Lead the way."

Claire had the girls working on their wand skills, and Josiah had moved to the third floor to observe and offer advice. "Give them a break, darling. They are not ready for wands. Teach them the broad strokes of Tarot and build up their self-esteem."

"Okay, Jos, if you think that's the way to go."

"What is *Monsieur* LeJeune saying?" asked Michele.

"He thinks the wands are taking too much of your energy at this early stage. He suggests I teach you the beginnings of Tarot today. Did each of you bring the deck you bought in the square?"

They had, and they pulled them out.

"First, each of you will cleanse and bless your deck. After we're finished, you'll place it in your velvet bag—not in the box the cards came in."

"There's so much to learn, my heart is pounding," said Charlotte.

"We'll start with the major arcana," said Claire, "and learn the interpretation of each of the cards." She retrieved her cards from a purple satin case she carried with her in her purse. "One card at a time. It's a lot to learn, and you'll need to refer to your notes for a long while, so make nicely detailed notes to help you in the future."

Their faces flushed with excitement, the girls opened their Tarot decks and got their notebooks ready.

Flemings Steakhouse, New Orleans

Misty scanned the wine list while Luke looked over the menu. She smiled up at the server and handed it back. "I'll try the house chianti. We need to celebrate my new black Expedition. Tomorrow, you'll be able to chauffer half the neighborhood."

Misty joked, but yes, the truck was big. Big enough for everyone and their stuff. The more important thing was that Luke liked it. Considering he'd be the one driving it more often, she was glad he'd been there to help choose it.

"I'll have a Miller draft," said Luke.

Misty reached across the table and touched his hand. "Thanks for your help at the dealership, sugar. I'm so happy you decided to come home. It's made all the difference for me."

Luke squeezed her fingers. "It's great to be back. I like the energy of your house and all the activity. It's hard to be lonely when there's always something happening."

"And we can still do police work whenever you want to. If that's something you enjoy, there are always people missing I could help find."

Luke accepted his beer from the server and waited for them to be alone again before speaking. "Did you get any vibes when you read over the murder case file?"

She tested the wine. It was lovely. "Not from reading reports, no. I need contact with something of the victims, or to visit the scene or the victim's home. Did you happen to notice how old the murders were?"

"Umm… no, but that's a good point. I'll check into that when we get home."

"Usually, the older they are, the less energy I'll sense. I don't want Lieutenant White to expect too much."

Luke shrugged. "We'll go and see where the magick takes you. That's all you can do."

Louis Armstrong Airport

Casey's flight landed at ten after ten in the evening. He came flying through the arrival doors with his duffel bag in his hand and his dark mop of hair flying. When he reached Misty, he dropped his bag and hugged her tightly. "Thank you for inviting me to stay with you. I'm so happy you're going to teach me, my Voodoo Queen. When Blaine told me, I almost imploded."

Misty giggled and eased back to give him a wink. "I'm glad you didn't implode. Is that all your luggage?"

"Oh, no, I have a big one too. I got so excited I just ran out and forgot."

Luke laughed. "Okay, we'll have to talk to someone and get you back in there for it."

Casey shrugged. "Yeah, sorry. I've never had so many clothes and stuff before Blaine found me."

"Did you bring your laptop?" asked Luke.

"Uh-huh. I think I brought everything I might need."

Misty chuckled at the boy's excitement. "Okay, let's find that suitcase and then get you home and settled. I want you looking fresh when you meet your classmates in the morning."

"Blaine said they were all girls."

Luke handed Casey his duffle, a big grin lighting up his handsome face. "Down boy. You're here to learn magick, not chase after older women."

Casey flashed a smile of his own. "Blaine says I'm good at multitasking."

CHAPTER TWELVE

Wednesday, January 11th.

Nine Saint Gillian Street

The next morning, Luke found Casey on the back porch smoking and watching Hoodoo bounce crazily around the yard. He joined him and pulled out his lighter. The kid was a runaway street rat Blaine found in the Gulf while he was on a case. Annie had given Blaine a home when he had none, and Blaine always tried to pay it forward.

"Hey, you're up early, kid," he said, lighting up and taking a long pull.

Casey's smile was infectious. "Too excited to sleep. I love New Orleans, and I have so much to learn. Misty brought me home with her before, you know, but she didn't clear it with Blaine. He was so fuckin pissed. It was unreal. I never had a home before, and nobody ever cared where I was. Blaine cares. He wants me safe and happy."

"He's a helluva good man. You'd do well to follow

his lead and mind what he teaches you."

"Yep. Trust me, I know it. Now that I'm all caught up on my schooling, I'm taking a course in criminology, and I help him out in the office sometimes when he's overloaded. Why are you here, Luke?"

He smiled. Casey could talk faster than anyone he knew. "Some weird stuff happened here at the house, and Misty was frightened. Two different people were trying to get her family grimoire."

"The LeJeune Book of Shadows?"

Luke nodded and exhaled a cloud of smoke. "Yep."

"Geeze, I looked through that book when she had it with her in Austin. It's amazing. All the old spells and stuff. Some of the pages are torn, and you have to handle it carefully. Are people still after the book?"

"One for sure. The other one, not so much." He glanced around for Wannabe. "Did you see a big frog by the fishpond?"

"No, but I saw Hoo chasing something into the herb garden earlier. Didn't see what it was."

Luke chuckled. "Probably Wannabe."

"Did Misty name a frog?"

"She did. The girls like him."

Mention of the girls brought another round of smiles to the kid's face. "I didn't know Misty was starting a school, but I'm glad she did. There aren't many ways to learn what I want to know unless someone teaches you one on one."

"Magick is passed down through generations. My

gran is a Hoodoo practitioner down south near Houma, and I grew up in her care. I know a few things, but only because I lived with her and watched everything she did."

"Lots of non-believers out there." Casey ground his smoke out under his boot, then picked up the butt. "But, I've seen Misty move things with her mind. That's called something. I saw her do it."

"Telekinesis," Luke said. "I'd love to see that."

"You could ask her."

"No, sir. Misty and those like her don't appreciate being asked to perform parlor tricks. It's considered rude and abuse of the power the goddess bestowed."

"Oh, good to know. Thanks, Luke. I'll be careful not to do that then. I don't want to piss her off in any way."

Breakfast at number nine Saint Gillian Street was becoming more of an event every day. Misty made blueberry waffles to celebrate Casey's arrival, and while they ate, her mother talked non-stop about her plans for the students. Misty got the distinct impression that she had been downgraded to a guest instructor, and that was fine. She was busy enough already.

"What did I miss on the first two days, Madam LeJeune?"

"I did a little testing with wands, and yesterday we began the Tarot. You haven't missed much. I can test you this morning before the girls arrive if you like. It would be good to know if you were born with any gifts."

"I'm not sure if I have any natural-born talent, but I have desire—a burning desire to learn magick ever since I first met Misty down at the gulf."

"Without the passion, nothing happens in life," her mother said. "Passion and focus are two excellent qualities to have."

After breakfast Misty took Casey out into the back garden to cut a piece of ash. He was keen to make his own wand before the girls arrived.

"How long should it be, Mist?" He was showing her about an eighteen-inch piece.

"Start with that, then trim off the ends and whittle it down until it feels right in your hand."

Casey cut the piece with Misty's athame and handed the knife back to her. He held the stick in his hand. "I can feel the energy."

"That's a good sign. Now you'll need to work with it and reveal its character. Take your time and develop a rapport."

"Like decorate it with crystals and shit, then make friends with it?"

Misty giggled. "Something like that."

"Will you show me?"

She nodded and pointed toward the back porch. "Let's go in. Angelique has a box of crystals. She might spare you a couple if you ask her nicely. I'll show you a couple of my father's old wands too, so you get the idea."

Claire took Casey to the third floor once he was satisfied that he and his wand had begun a strong working relationship. It could take ages to perfect a wand, but a connection had to be there from the start. She showed him the classroom. "You can sit here at the end of the table. The girls already have spots claimed where they like to sit."

"Can't wait to meet them."

"A couple are older than you are by a couple of years, but I believe Diana is around your age."

"I'm seventeen."

She nodded. "A perfect age to begin serious study. Shall we try your wand before the girls come?"

"Yeah, let's try before they get here. I don't want them laughing at me if I crash and burn."

"Hold it in your dominant hand and imagine that you're sending your energy down your arm, out your fingers, and through the wand."

"Do I have to say magick words?"

Claire smiled at his endless enthusiasm. "No, this is only a test. Don't think of anything else, and don't let your mind wander. Try hard to focus on what you're doing. Breathe in and focus on harnessing the energy within you."

Casey closed his eyes, and she could feel the potential building within him. A few moments later, a white fireball flew out the end of the wand, whizzed past her head, and hit the wall about a foot from the burnt patch where Charlotte's fire landed two days earlier.

Claire jumped up and smothered the fire on the wallpaper with her charred broom. "That was impressive, young man. A wonderful first try."

"Whoa, did I do that?"

She chuckled. "You definitely did."

"Yahoo. I'm pumped."

The girls stampeded up the steps and into the classroom while she was still putting out the smoldering wall. They sat down in their seats, and Claire made the introductions. "Girls, this is Casey, Misty's young friend she told you about. And Casey, this is Diana, Charlotte, and Michele."

Casey grinned. "Hey. I'm so happy to be here with y'all. This is going to be a blast."

"Welcome to school, Casey," said Diana. "Do you have any special gifts?"

"I don't know yet, but I'm hoping I do. I've only had one test so far." He glanced at the second burnt spot on the wall.

"Oh, you set the paper on fire like Char did," said Diana. "How cool is that?"

Michele didn't seem to agree.

Charlotte zoned in on the whittled stick in Casey's hand. "Is that your wand?"

"Misty and Angelique helped me make it this morning. It's not done yet, but ain't it cool?"

Charlotte nodded. "I'd like to make my own too."

Claire headed them off before she lost control. "We'll be making personal wands in the next day or two. Start to think about your designs and how y'all wish to embellish them: crystals, carvings, sigils, or whatever else y'all fancy."

"I want crystals on mine like Casey," said Diana. "Did you write your letter to say what you most want to do with magick?"

Casey shook his head. "No. I just got here last night. But, if I had to say it would be moving things with my mind like Misty. It's so freaking cool when she does that."

Claire rolled her eyes and doubled her effort to rein them in. "Diana, dear, would you get Casey a notebook and pen from the cupboard, please. And Michele, grab one of the extra decks of cards in drawer that Casey can use until he chooses his own."

Luke hibernated in his room after breakfast and worked on researching the past and present of their mysterious Linc Castille. The man's motives behind his interest in Misty's book were cloudy and needed to be clarified if he was to be stopped. His instincts told him the answers lay in the man's family tree.

Searching through dozens of families in Louisiana bearing the Castille name, it took a while to find the right one. Finding a Lincoln Castille whose father had owned and operated a security business was easy enough.

The trick was to find something more profound.

After an hour of diligent searching, he came across something that sparked his interest. The woman who raised Linc wasn't his biological mother. According to his birth records, he was born to a Tilly Castille from Houma. Aha, there were a lot of powerful magickals with roots in Houma.

"I wonder if Gran knows her."

With the woman's name discovered, he had a fairly good idea why Linc wanted the book. Now he needed the evidence to back him off and end this.

His cell rang, and Luke didn't recognize the number. It was a local number, though, and he was waiting for a callback from Lieutenant White. "Luke Hyslop."

"Yes, Ranger Hyslop, I have a message here that you tried to get me yesterday. Was it regarding Madam LeJeune helping with the case?"

Luke sat back in his desk chair. "Yes, sir, she'd like to visit the residence of the first victim with you and me in attendance. Can you arrange that?"

"I can. I'm delighted she's willing to help."

"I needn't remind you that she doesn't want your partner involved. She doesn't trust him, and we both know her instincts aren't to be questioned."

"Ellis isn't a bad man, Mr. Hyslop. He's God-fearing and has an understandable prejudice where magick is involved."

Luke bristled. "There are no understandable prejudices, Lieutenant. Especially against a woman as open and generous as Misty LeJeune."

"No, sir. You're right. I apologize for saying it like that. And yes, I understand. Madam LeJeune's involvement will remain between the three of us. I'll call you back as soon as I have the visit set up."

Luke found Angelique conducting a lesson on doll magick when he came downstairs to the kitchen. Casey and the girls were staring at her in wide-eyed wonder as she explained the basics. He wondered if it was the subject matter that had them so focused or their attempts to understand the native woman's thick Cajun dialect.

Misty was busy with labels and checking things off lists over on the far counter. He went to her and leaned in, trying not to interrupt the lesson. "Hey, it's time to pick up the Expedition. Are you able to leave now?"

"Oh," she said, blinking up at him. "I forgot about that. Yes, I'll get my coat."

During the ride to the Ford dealership, Luke filled her in on what he found out about Linc Castille.

"He wants the book for his mother?"

"That's my guess. She was listed as living in Houma. When I checked with the records department, the property remains registered in her name."

"Road trip," said Misty. "We'll take everyone for a ride in the new truck tomorrow, and I'll speak to her."

"Are you sure that's the way to handle it?"

"Why beat around the bush? I'll go straight to her and see what kind of vibes I get from her."

Luke didn't like the idea of Misty putting herself in

harm's way. "I know you're strong, but I'm still worried. We don't know anything about this woman or what she's capable of."

Misty reached over and squeezed Luke's thigh. "And Linc Castille and his mother don't know what I'm capable of either. It's sweet that you're worried about me, sugar. I appreciate it. Let's play it by ear and see what happens."

Ford Dealership

Luke parked the blue Honda in one of the visitor parking spots against the building and reached for the door handle. He noticed Misty's cd case attached to the visor, and it reminded him. "We should've cleaned out your car before we came."

"Oops, okay, let me have a look around." Misty peeked in the glove box and took out a plastic bag of dog biscuits. "These aren't mine."

Luke smiled. "I'll check the trunk and under the seats. Who knows what other treasures we might find."

Misty rolled her eyes at him, and he laughed. Man, when was the last time he'd laughed with a woman without feeling guilt and grief squeezing the air from his lungs? Far too long.

And then there was the other physical response to a woman he'd denied himself for far too long.

Misty was a *very* attractive woman.

He adjusted the front of his jeans and popped the trunk. There were three plastic bags of miscellaneous stuff. He collected the handles and gathered everything up. "Okay, all clear back here. You'll have to look through these bags when we get home."

Misty eyed the bags and shrugged. "Obviously, I haven't missed any of that, because I don't even know what's in those."

Misty finished paying for the truck, signed the purchase agreement, and the salesperson handed her the keys.

Luke flipped through the manual while she finished that. "The maintenance package is included with your purchase. So we have to bring the truck in when the system alerts us."

She dangled the key in front of him and smiled. "I hereby turn that task over to you. Enjoy your new ride, cowboy."

"Thanks, I will." Luke slid behind the wheel, and his cell rang. "Lieutenant White?"

"I have the first visit set up for Madam LeJeune. Would one o'clock be convenient?"

Luke gazed at Misty across the console. "One o'clock, okay for a site visit?"

She nodded.

"One will be fine. Could you text me the address? We're out, and the files are back at Misty's."

Bakery Café

Luke parked behind the café Misty directed him to. He turned off the rumble of the engine and rounded the hood of the truck in time to help Misty down from the sidestep. "I take it that you've been to this bakery before?"

"One of my favorites. Let's sit inside. That wind is cool."

Luke ushered her inside and rubbed her arms while they waited for a server to point them to a table. "You should have worn a heavier jacket."

"My head is usually in the clouds. As a rule, things like the thickness of my jacket lining is an afterthought once I'm already freezing."

Luke chuckled. "Doesn't matter. We have half an hour, and hot coffee to warm you up."

When they were settled, Misty took his hand and smiled. "I'm glad you're helping me with the murder cases. I admit, I'm a little nervous. What if I make a mistake?"

"You won't. You'll see and feel what's there. The police can interpret your information any way they care to."

Misty exhaled. "Thank you. It's nice to have someone calm and logical in my life to keep me grounded. I don't get much of that from my parents, as you might have noticed."

Luke chuckled. "The LeJeunes are definitely unique."

Misty burst into laughter.

"But seriously," he said, "I think you've done pretty well on your own. You're just overwhelmed."

They accepted their order of coffee and sugared baguettes, and Misty grew serious. "Three murders. Do you really think the killer might be a woman?"

"Poison is traditionally a woman's weapon."

"Well, I can't say I'm looking forward to what I find today. Death can carry terrible energy."

Luke set his mug down on the table. "You can always opt-out. You're helping the police do *their* job. I'm not in favor of you stressing over it. You've been through enough with what's going on at the house."

South Ward, New Orleans

Misty was filled with apprehension as Luke parked behind Lieutenant White's unmarked in the first victim's driveway. The bungalow was newly built, small and neat with a perfectly trimmed yard.

"Someone's been cutting the grass," said Luke as he gave Misty a hand out of the passenger door. "Hey, you're shaking. Are you sure you want to do this?"

"I'll be okay. Can you grab my water?"

"Sure." He checked that she was steady and then reached in to grab one of the bottles they'd picked up earlier."

Misty hesitated on the front step, and Luke looked like he was about to voice a protest to doing this when White opened the door and welcomed them in.

"I'm glad y'all could make it today. Please come in."

"Does anyone live here now?" asked Misty.

"Mr. Baird's girlfriend was living here, but she moved back with her family after his death."

Misty nodded. "I can see how upsetting it would be for her to stay here."

"Where would you like to start, Madam?"

Misty gave the interior a look. "I'll do a walkthrough first to see if anything overt comes to me, then possibly sit in his bedroom and touch his clothes or jewelry for a few minutes. Items worn close to the body for long periods carry the most residual energy."

"Would you like to do this alone?"

"Luke will stay with me in case I feel faint."

"I'll wait out here," said White and sat down on the sofa.

Misty started in the kitchen and noticed how clean and neat it was. Perhaps someone had cleaned up after the forensic people. They always made an ungodly mess. A quick turn through the adjoining dining area took her through the living room, and then down the short hallway to the two bedrooms. She headed into the larger of the two.

She sat on the side of the bed and tried to get a sense of the man who'd slept in this room. She'd seen his picture in the file, but only in death. Dark hair and slim build.

She stood, walked over to the dresser, and looked at the items still waiting for his return. Tie bar. A small pile of change. A picture of a pretty girl with long, honey-blonde hair.

Drawn to the closet, Misty opened the door and gasped. Death wrapped around her so tightly she almost smothered. She stepped away and caught her breath.

Luke's arm came around her waist as he hugged her to his side. His strength and the warmth from his body were the only things that kept her from fainting.

"The closet," she mumbled.

"What does that mean?"

She tried to articulate what she'd felt a moment ago, but even thinking of it had her near to fainting. Luke scooped her into his arms and carried her over to the bed. "Here, Misty, look at me. Take a sip of water."

After a couple of sips, he sat her up. "There's something in the closet."

"Okay. Let's get you out of here. You can wait in the front room, and Lieutenant White and I will take the closet on."

Misty nodded.

Luke helped her into the living room, and they clued in the Lieutenant.

"You're saying forensics missed something in the closet?"

"I don't know," said Misty. "I don't know what I felt, just the overwhelming impression of death."

"Can't hurt to have another look," said Luke.

He and White were gone a long while, which suited Misty fine. She curled up on her side and rested on the couch. When they came back, Luke held up a plastic evidence bag with a business card from Kellerman's

Jewelry Store.

"We searched the closet itself, as well as every pocket in every suit and shirt, and every shoe. The only thing we came up with was this." Luke held the card towards her, and Misty pulled her hand back.

"Throw away the latex gloves and wash your hands, Luke. I feel a connection to poison on that."

Luke did as she asked and came back to gather her from the sofa. "I'm taking you home. That's enough for one day."

"Thank you so much, Madam," said White. "I'll put every effort into connecting this card to Mr. Baird's murder."

Nine Saint Gillian Street

Misty was lying down in her bedroom recovering from her outing when her cell rang. Tired and still disoriented, she didn't bother checking the screen. "Hello."

"Madam LeJeune, this is Detective Ellis. I'm calling to thank you for my broken foot. I know you did it."

"Why Detective Ellis, you don't believe in me or magick. Whatever could I have done?"

"If I had any evidence, I'd bring charges against you."

"And I'd bring harassment charges against you. I cast a protection spell to ward against anyone untrustworthy or treacherous. The fact that you couldn't cross that barrier says more about you than it does me."

"This isn't over, LeJeune."

"Are you threatening me, Ellis? Because if you are, I'll make it my life's mission to expose you and have you removed from the police force. If you know what's good for you, you'll stay out of my way."

Misty pressed *end*, and started to cry.

The chair in Luke's room brushed the floor, and a moment later, he filled the doorframe of her bedroom.

"Ellis is mad about his broken foot."

"And you, my lady, are exhausted. Give me that." He took the phone from her hand. "Now get some rest."

She shrugged. "It's hard to relax. Sometimes it feels like everyone is coming at me from all sides: Ellis, Linc, Fabian."

Luke frowned, crawled onto her bed, and pulled her against his chest. After adjusting her hair and blankets, she rested her head on his arm. "Close your eyes and get some rest. No one will come at you while I'm on the job. You're safe."

He kissed her lightly on the forehead, and she closed her eyes, more content than she had been in ages. Yes. She was so thankful to have Luke in her life.

The Apartment, New Orleans

"Who thinks Casey is adorably cute?" asked Diana.

"He's cute all right," said Charlotte, "but he's seventeen. He's yours for the taking, Diana."

"He's not mine," said Diana. "That's silly."

Michele rolled her eyes. "Know what we should

do?"

"What?"

"Make that love potion and give it to Cascy. It would make him crazy hot for Diana."

Diana screamed. "Don't. Don't do that. I beg you."

Michele laughed. "It might put some fun into your life."

"I have too much fun already."

Charlotte pointed the remote at her and waved it like a wand. "No, you don't. You need a boyfriend."

"From what I saw of your last boyfriend, that's the last thing anyone needs. He hit you."

Charlotte smiled a cunning smile. "And when I learn how, I'll cast something on him for payback."

"He deserves it," said Michele. "Now back to Casey and Diana. How are we going to make that happen?"

CHAPTER THIRTEEN

Thursday, January 12th.

<u>Nine Saint Gillian Street</u>

As soon as the girls arrived for classes, Misty informed them about the road trip to Houma. That set off a round of squealing, which, in turn, got a hilarious, wide-eyed look from Casey. She supposed he hadn't experienced the full force of the girls' excitement.

"Come into the kitchen," her mother said, waving them in from the front hall. "Each of you will prepare your gathering basket. I've cut some ribbon for y'all to decorate your baskets with your personal colors."

The girls were attentive as they watched her mother tie the colored ribbons to her basket in demonstration. "Each of you will need a bolline to properly harvest the plants and roots, and a gift to leave the goddess thanking her for her generosity."

"I have several bollines in the drying hutch in the back yard," said Misty. "Nice and sharp, and I'll show you how to cut the plants and roots when it's time.

We're only looking for what we need. Nothing more."

"I don't know how to tell one plant from the other," said Casey. "I only know vegetables from pulling weeds in Carm's garden, and I could pick out a pot plant if we came across one."

That made the girls laugh.

Misty couldn't help but laugh too. She adored Casey. "You're right. We should have had a lesson on that before the trip, but I need to see someone down that way so we're improvising. We'll play it by ear this first time."

"Do we have a list of what we need?" asked Charlotte.

Her mother distributed a basket to each of them. "Yes, Angelique has it for you."

Misty packed a little cooler with drinks and zipped that up on the counter. "We'll call on Luke's gran, Madam Hyslop, and take a short trek along the bayou to see what we can find. I need to make one other stop, and perhaps we'll have time to shop in a couple of stores I like to frequent in Houma."

"Should we bring our notebooks?" asked Charlotte.

Misty nodded. "Definitely, bring notebooks and pens. "This will be an educational field trip, like in a regular school, only we'll learn things they never teach."

When they were ready to leave, Hoodoo bounced around them in circles, whining to go with them.

"Are we taking Hoo?" asked Casey, shrugging into his leather jacket.

"Not this time. I think he should stay here with Mother and Angelique. He's a good watchdog."

Her mother chuckled, waving away her words. "We'll be fine without the dog, Misty. In fact, we might have a peaceful day without him."

Misty knew her mother could take care of herself, but still worried. "Alright, Hoo can come."

"Shall we take Wannabe to the swamp with us?" asked Luke, pointing a thumb over his shoulder. "He'd be much happier there."

"Nooo," said the girls in chorus.

Michele stuck her lip out, looking particularly put out by the idea. "He's so cute in the yard. I love watching him hop. Does he have to go?"

"He should go," said Luke. "For his own good."

"*Oui*, I'll put him in a bucket," said Angelique, hurrying toward the back door. "He must go."

Misty nodded. "He'll have friends there. It's for the best."

"Aw," said Michele. "I'll sit beside him in the truck and talk to him."

"You speak frog?" asked Casey.

Michele stared. "I have a rapport with animals."

"He's an amphibian," said Casey.

"Well, aren't you smart?" asked Michele with an edge to her voice.

"My guardian is a genius," said Casey. "It rubs off."

"Why do you have a guardian?" asked Michele.

"Don't you have parents?"

"Nope." Casey turned his head and stared out the window.

Little Diana sitting beside him, reached for his hand. "Ignore Michele. She's being nosy. It's nice that you have a guardian who's smart and watches out for you. You're lucky."

Casey nodded. "Yeah. Thanks."

Houma, Louisiana

An hour later, Luke drove their little band of misfits into Houma. "Anybody want a coffee or a bathroom break before we carry on to the wilds of the swamp?"

"Both would be wonderful," said Misty, "What about the rest of y'all?"

"Uh-huh," said Charlotte. "I think I'll get a Coke."

"I put Cokes in the cooler."

"Yeah, we drank them already."

Misty blinked at the backseat. "Okay, then definitely we'll need to take a bathroom break. There's no port-a-potties in the swamp, girls. If you need to pee, it's behind a tree with snakes and spiders."

The look on their faces was priceless.

When everyone was refreshed and armed with drinks and snacks, Luke drove out of town. It had been too long since he'd been home. But as he followed the twists and turns on the backroads he grew up on, he realized it was time.

Life hadn't gone the way he'd planned. He'd lost his wife and his baby girl, but that was in the past. He needed to get back to his roots and start living again.

When he finally stopped in front of the small wooden house on the edge of the bayou, he knew he'd made the right call in coming home.

"Does your Gran know we're coming?" asked Misty.

"She has no phone. It will be a surprise."

They all spilled out of the truck, and Hoo was happy to be free. He bounced around barking and turning in circles.

"Don't run away, Hoo," said Casey.

An old woman with long white hair opened the door and stepped outside, pulling her shawl tighter around her against the dampness. She took in the group, and then her gaze locked on him. A smile curved her lips, and he felt a sudden wave of guilt for staying away so long. "Lukey, is that you?"

"It's me, Gran." He wrapped his arms around her and held her in a long hug. "I missed you so much."

"Is this your family?" she asked.

He stepped back and held his hand out for Misty to join them. "This is Madam Misty LeJeune."

"Oh, my." Luke's grandmother bent her knee slightly and dropped her gaze. "This is an honor to have you visit, Madam."

Misty took her hand and was as warm and kind as Luke knew she would be. "I'm happy to meet you,

Madam. Luke has told me wonderful tales of growing up here in the bayou."

"Come in, children. I have tea on the stove."

After tea and cookies with Luke's grandmother, Misty led the way along the bank of the bayou, referred to Angelique's list, and pointed to different plants and roots they should gather.

"Draw a circle around the plant before you cut it and say thank you to each plant for providing you with what you need."

When the harvesting ended, the girls placed their full baskets carefully in the back of the truck. Luke picked up the bucket and held it out. "Who wants to let Mr. Wannabe go?"

"I will," said Michele. "Although it breaks my heart."

"My gran will be here with him," said Luke. "She'll take good care of him, I promise."

As Luke passed the bucket off, his gran's attention locked on the frog and then turned to him. Luke chuckled. "Don't ask. Needless to say, Misty's not one to go after with ill intent."

His gran seemed to accept that.

Michele trudged to the edge of the water and dumped the frog out of the bucket. "Be free, Wannabe. We will miss you."

As everybody piled into the truck to leave, Wannabe hopped away from the bank and followed them.

"Aww . . . he doesn't want us to go," said Michele.

"He'll get over it," said Misty.

Luke chuckled, and programmed Tilly Castille's address into the GPS. Following directions, he turned onto the road and headed back to Houma. They arrived at her small brick house twenty minutes later.

"Everyone stays in the truck," Misty said, releasing the buckle of her seatbelt. "I won't be long."

Luke jumped out of the truck to accompany her, and she shook her head. "I can do this."

"I know you *can*, but Linc has proven to be duplicitous and dangerous. We don't know if his mother is controlling him or influencing him. And we don't know how powerful a witch she is. I'm coming with you."

After a moment of considering his argument, Misty nodded. Together, they walked up the path and knocked on the purple door.

A tall, black-haired woman in her late fifties opened the door and peered at them through wire-rimmed glasses. "Yes?"

"Madam Castille?"

"Yes."

"I'm Mystere LeJeune. I need to speak to you about your son, Lincoln."

The woman's eyes grew wide, and she tried to close the door. "Stay away from me."

Luke got the toe of his boot in the door before it closed and pushed it open. Misty and he entered the house and found themselves standing in the living room.

Luke closed the door and took a long look at the woman. "The way you just reacted. You must be aware of what Linc is up to."

The woman milled her hands together, looking both afraid and furious. "Lincoln does what he does. He lives in the city. He's his own man."

"Madam Castille," said Misty. "As a woman of the craft, you, of all people, must understand that my family's Book of Shadows is something I will fight to protect. The wisdom on those pages belongs to the LeJeune family, and those we see fit to share it with. Nothing good will come to anyone who tries to take it by force or deception."

"It's Lincoln who wants it," the woman said. "I told him it was too dangerous even to think about, but he is obsessed."

"Why does he want it?" asked Luke.

"He was born with power and raised by a man who thinks anything in life is his for the taking. Lincoln feels he has a right to learn from not only a great book, but the *greatest* book."

Misty shook her head. "Please try to talk him out of it, Madam. It would be in his best interest."

The woman held out her shaking hands. "Please, don't hurt him, Madam LeJeune. He's a good boy. He doesn't realize what he's doing."

Misty frowned. "Oh, I think he knows very well what he's doing, Madam. I'll put a stop to it if I must, but it would be better for everyone if it didn't come to that."

With that, Misty turned to him. "We better go."

As Luke leaned in to open Misty's door for her, he sensed her tension. "What is it? She seemed alright."

"No. That entire conversation was an act. You were right, that woman holds far more power than I gave her credit for."

"Okay, what does that mean?"

"It means, I should've picked up on Linc's power."

"And you didn't."

She shook her head. "If he's strong enough to block me, there's no telling what he's capable of. We need to get back to nine Saint Gillian, right now."

Nine Saint Gillian Street

Claire was busy working with Angelique in the kitchen when a shuffle in the front foyer had them both pausing. Angelique, pointed as if to question that she'd heard the same thing, and Claire nodded. She picked up her wand and put it into the pocket of her apron, then proceeded down the hall.

Linc Castille stood in the foyer, doing something to the security panel just inside the door.

"Mr. Castille, however did you get in this house?"

Linc closed the panel and laughed. "You mean, how did I sidestep your warding? Please, I anticipated that days before you caught on enough to start protecting yourself."

Claire ran through the possibilities in her head and didn't like any of them. "You've planted hex bags somewhere in the house—a back door to sidestep our wards."

Linc winked at her. "Now you're catching on. Now, tell me, where do you LeJeunes hide your Book of Shadows?"

Claire forced a laugh and edged her hand into the pocket of her apron. "Get out of this house, Castille. If you're lucky, I'll call the police. If you're not, it'll go much worse for you."

Linc whipped out a wand, and before she could counter or defend, she slammed backward. Pinned to the wall behind her, she was frozen in place.

Linc sauntered up to her struggling against his magick and swore by all the power in her veins she would wipe that smug smile off his face. "Tell me where the book is, Claire."

Claire spat at him, and Angelique came hard and fast, swinging a butcher's knife. Claire couldn't make out most of the words Angelique was firing at him, but caught, "gut you like d'a pig you are."

Linc dropped his wand to catch Angelique's arm. She was a big woman and had a lot of fight. He twisted her wrist, and the knife clattered to the floor.

> *Blackest cats with nine of lives*
> *Eating rodents, you survive*
> *Gardens growing greenest chives*
> *I cast your body dowsed in hives*

172 · AUBURN TEMPEST

Claire smiled at the puff of smoke and the voice of her husband coming to their rescue. She dropped to her feet and drew her wand, throwing a repulsion spell at Linc that had him toppling end over end toward the open front door.

"Get out of this house," she snapped, smiling at Castille scratching and tearing at his skin as he ran down the walk.

"Thank you, darling," Claire said, blowing a kiss toward the ghost of her husband hovering by the entrance to the kitchen. "I'll consider a stronger protection spell for the house. You need to find whatever hex bags or nasty little tricks that man planted. He had access to this house for two days. There's no telling what else he's done."

"Consider it done, my love."

Claire took Angelique by the arm and eased her toward the kitchen. "Come, dear, we need to put salve on your wrist where that dreadful man hurt you."

Misty's anxiety was getting away from her by the time Luke stopped to drop the girls off on the way back home. As much as she wanted to race straight there, if there was trouble, the last thing she wanted was for the girls to be caught in the middle.

But once Luke pulled into her spot behind the house, Misty was out of her seat and racing inside. The negative energy hit her like a hammer the moment she opened the door.

She ran into the main hall and reeled backward. "Mother! Angelique! Where are you? Are you all right?"

Claire rushed up the hall from the kitchen. She looked a little haggard, but whole. "We're fine, darling. Your fellow, Mr. Castille, came by a short time ago. He's gone now."

"He came into the house?" Luke said. "How?"

"He did something to the panel, to bypass the system," said Claire. "As well, he'd placed counter-spells within the house to allow him to evade our ward. Josiah is sure he's found them all, but he's taking one more look, to be sure."

"I'm calling the police," said Luke.

"Did he hurt you or Angelique, Mother?"

Claire sighed. "He hurt Angelique's wrist, and gave me a rude awakening, but no. It was mostly a bad fright for us both."

"What about Daddy?"

"Josiah saved the day, as usual. He cast that itching spell he loves to use."

Misty's tension eased some then. "The crazy one that causes an infestation of hives?"

"That's the one. Linc Castille is covered in hives."

Luke grinned, his phone against his ear. "Officers will be along shortly to take your statements. Then they'll arrest Linc Castille for trespassing and assault."

Misty headed to the kitchen and pulled a bottle of

red from the wine cooler. For Casey and Luke, she grabbed two beers. When she handed Casey his, she locked gazes. "When the police arrive, you better not still have this in your hand."

Casey gave her a nod and twisted off the cap. "What about attempted robbery?"

Luke lowered his bottle and swallowed. "I don't think he got that far. Did he, ladies?"

Misty's mother shook her head. "He demanded to know where Misty kept the book. His intent was evident, but I don't know if that counts."

"We'll see what the police think."

Misty poured herself a glass of wine and then poured two more. "Mother, you and Angelique both deserve to unwind a bit after that."

Claire chuckled. "Perhaps we should wait until after we speak to the police. In the meantime, did you speak to Madam Castille, Mystere?"

"Yes. She swore the idea to steal the book is all Linc and had nothing to do with her."

"Did you believe her?"

Misty looked at Luke. "She sounded convincing, but my instincts say no. She's more dangerous than she wants us to realize."

The police arrived twenty minutes later and took statements from Misty's mother and Angelique. When they'd wrapped that up, they spoke to her about Linc and his work within the house while installing the security system. They sent word that a car had been sent to locate Linc, and he would be picked up as soon as they found him.

Misty walked them to the door. "You might want to check hospitals, clinics, or infirmaries around his home. I have it on good authority he might be suffering a terrible case of hives."

"That's a never-fail spell," said Josiah from his corner of the kitchen. "The wording could use a little tweaking, but the result is always fantastic."

"You're funny, Daddy," said Misty, joining them and pouring herself a second glass of wine. "I'm too tired to cook dinner. Let's order pizza."

Casey smiled. "You read my mind, my voodoo princess."

CHAPTER FOURTEEN

Friday, January 13th.

<u>Nine Saint Gillian Street</u>

Luke was enjoying breakfast with Misty and Casey when Claire whisked in. "This will surely be a lucky day," she said. "Good things always happen on Friday the 13th.

He chuckled. "We'll be lucky if Linc Castille isn't granted bail. I'm going to his arraignment at nine-thirty."

"I'll come with you," said Misty.

Luke ran a finger around the rim of his coffee cup, searching for the right way to put Misty off. "I'd rather you didn't. He'll be furious with you and might be openly hostile. I don't want you subjected to more of his abuse."

Misty frowned. "He must realize by now his behavior is getting him into trouble."

Casey finished his second plate of bacon and pancakes and took his plate to the sink. "Can I come? I want to see the hives."

"You have classes in an hour, young man," Claire

said. "Everything we harvested yesterday has to be hung and preserved. We can't let any of it go to waste."

Casey shrugged. "Okay, I'll stay here and help the girls. I don't want them mad at me."

"Smart man," Luke said.

"Yeah, I don't think Michele likes me much as it is."

Luke's cell rang. He checked the screen and stepped out onto the back porch to answer. "Yes, Lieutenant White? What can I do for you?"

"We followed up on the card found in Nelson Baird's closet, and it seems he bought an engagement ring for his girlfriend at the jewelry store just before he died."

"Nothing else?" asked Luke.

"That's all we've got so far. We're checking to see if either of the other victims did something similar."

"Thanks for keeping me updated."

"You're welcome. I also called to ask if Madam LeJeune would consider visiting the second victim's residence."

Luke wasn't keen on that at all, but that wasn't his call to make. "I'll ask her and give you a call if she's willing to try."

"Thank you, Ranger Hyslop."

Misty smiled as Luke returned from outside. "You have a funny look on your face. Is Wannabe back in the yard?"

Luke chuckled. "No, nothing that magickal.

Lieutenant White is asking you to go to the second victim's residence."

Misty stiffened, and he regretted bringing it up. "Did he follow up on the jewelry store card?"

"He says there was nothing nefarious, but the victim did buy an engagement ring there before he was murdered. He's still following up on that and cross-referencing to the other victims. After seeing how you reacted to that card, I bet they find something."

She hoped so. "One disaster at a time. Let's go see what Linc Castille is up to at the courthouse."

"Take care of yourself, dear," said Claire. "Don't let that criminal upset you any further."

Misty could hear her father chuckling in the corner of the kitchen. It was an eerie sound that gave her shivers. "Yeah, and take him some lotion for his hives."

After Luke and Misty left for the courthouse, the girls arrived for classes. Claire met them in the foyer. "Put your backpacks down for the moment, girls. Josiah and I have come up with a more potent protection spell for the house. That nasty man, Linc Castille, caused us a bit of trouble yesterday, and we're going to put a stop to it."

"Oh, what are we going to use?" asked Diana. "More castor beans?"

"This time, we're going with poke root tea. Angelique has brewed a big cauldron of it, and we're going to sprinkle it in all the doorways and corners of the house while we say the magick words."

"What are the magick words, Madam LeJeune?" Charlotte pulled out her notebook to jot down the spell.

"Josiah, what are the words to the one you wanted to try, dear?" asked Claire.

> *Protect this house from all sides*
> *Evil wash away in tides*
> *Evildoers stop and wait*
> *Stay outside our garden gate*
> *So mote it be*

"Thank you, dear. That's lovely. Got that, girls? Casey?"

They shook their heads. Right. They didn't hear Josiah talking, at least not yet. "I'll repeat it for you. Each of you take a bowl of the poke root tea and do all the rooms in the whole house. When you finish we'll join hands, and all say the spell together."

Angelique ladled tea into bowls and handed one to each of the four students.

"I'm excited we're doing a real spell," said Michele. "I hope it works, and that Castille man stays away."

"It will work," said Claire. "Most of Josiah's spells do."

New Orleans Courthouse

Misty and Luke sat near the front with the other three visitors in the courtroom. Arraignments weren't newsworthy events, and spectators rarely bothered unless it was a high profile case and had a widespread interest, or they knew one or both of the people involved.

"Are the cases in any particular order?" asked Misty.

Luke reached his arm around her shoulder and leaned close to whisper to her. "I'm not sure how they organize their docket. Usually, they list things by number, and the clerk calls the number."

"I've never been to an arraignment before."

Luke smiled. "I've been to many in Austin for people the agency had under surveillance."

They sat there together, and Misty wasn't so distracted that she didn't notice that even though the proceedings had begun, Luke left his arm across the back of her chair. As they watched the cases called, he played absently with a piece of her hair.

It was a small thing, but it made her feel very safe.

Another case number was called, and the bailiff brought Linc Castille into the courtroom with his lawyer. He was covered in red blotches and open sores. Misty had to cover her mouth to keep from laughing.

They stood in front of the judge while the clerk read the charges. "Mr. Castille, you are charged with breaking and entering, trespassing, attempted robbery, and two counts of assault."

"How do you plead?" asked the judge.

"Not guilty," Linc said.

"Your plea has been entered," said the judge.

"On the matter of bail," said his attorney, "Mr.

Castille has no police record. He is a local business owner and not a flight risk, Your Honor."

"So noted," said the judge. "Bail is granted in the amount of ten thousand dollars."

The bailiff escorted them out of the courtroom to arrange the bond.

"That's it?" asked Misty.

Luke shrugged. "That's your excitement for today."

Misty supposed they should have left, but Linc getting set free, like a normal person, made her angry. They were loitering in the parking lot when Linc Castille emerged with his lawyer. She wanted him to see her, wanted him to know that she was watching him.

When he did see her, he came running. "You did this, you evil witch. Take this spell off me, or you'll be sorry. I'll burn your witch house down and destroy you."

Luke pressed the fob and pushed her behind him. "Get in the truck, Misty."

Misty jumped into the front seat of the truck and locked her door. She watched Luke turn and face Linc.

"Mr. Castille, if you come near Madam LeJeune or Saint Gillian Street we'll have you arrested again. I'm warning you."

"You can warn me all you want. You can't control me."

Luke spoke to the lawyer standing behind Linc. "Sir, take your client home and make him listen to some sound advice."

"Come on, Linc. Let's go."

"I wish I had my wand with me," shouted Linc.

Luke slid behind the wheel of the truck. "We need a restraining order. I'll call Blacky as soon as we get home."

Misty knew all about restraining orders. She'd had one years ago when her husband used to hit her. She didn't think about Brad too much anymore.

That subject was dead and buried—like him.

On the way back home to Saint Gillian Street, Luke brought up the subject of the murders. "I don't like the idea of you going to the second victim's house, Misty. Those visions weaken you, and you've got enough going on right now."

Misty shrugged. "I feel guilty if I don't help."

"Well, let White work out the lead about the purchase at the jewelry store, and you can talk it over with your parents. See what they have to say."

Misty winked at him. "You're a sweet man, Lukey."

Luke laughed. "A man can't be held accountable for what his grandmother calls him."

Misty shrugged. "Aww, no, I think Lukey is cute."

Algiers Point

After a persuasive talk to her daughter, Claire convinced Misty that she would be the one to go to the second victim's residence. They would compare notes when Luke brought her home.

Reluctantly, Misty agreed and stayed home with

Josiah, Angelique, and the students.

Lieutenant White's unmarked vehicle was parked in the driveway of the two-story brick townhome when they arrived, and the man stood on the front porch waiting for them.

Opening the door, she gave Luke a reassuring glance. "Don't look so worried, Mr. Hyslop. All is well."

Nine Saint Gillian Street

Misty ushered Casey and the three girls to the third-floor classroom. "While Mother isn't here, we'll continue to work on the Tarot. It's a subject I know best, and y'all will need to be experts before we allow you to graduate."

"Will I be good enough to give readings when I graduate?" asked Diana.

Misty nodded. "Of course, you will. All it takes is practice, a knowledge of what each card means, and a natural intuition to help you interpret those meanings. Now, let's start with the four suits."

"Cups, wands, swords, and pentacles," Diana said.

"And the elemental and representation for each suit?"

Michele held up a card. "Cups is water and refers to emotion and feelings."

She looked at Charlotte next. "Wands are fire and deal with inspiration."

"Pentacles are the earth cards," Diana said. "They deal with stability and the physical world."

She looked to Case to finish them off, but he wasn't paying attention. "Hey, Case, what's up?"

Casey pointed out the window. "A man is trying to get the back gate open, and he can't. He looks crazy."

Misty rushed over to see. "That's Linc Castille. He's trying to climb over the fence. Daddy help, Linc's trying to get in here again."

"Do not despair, Mystere. The spell is protecting the house. Nothing he tries will hurt you."

"Call the police, Casey," Misty said, before running down the two sets of stairs, the long hallway, and out through the sunroom. She arrived at the back of the house in time to see Linc hurl himself over the fence. He landed in the yard, stumbled, and fell face-first into the fishpond.

Misty laughed and pulled her wand out of the pocket. She pointed it at Linc as he tried to climb out of the pond.

Swim with the fish
Splash and splish
Swim all day
Until I say
Frown and pout
You can't come out
So mote it be

The girls were clustered behind her and heard the spell. "Do you think he'll stay in the pond?" asked Charlotte.

Misty nodded. "He should. At least long enough until the police get here."

"I hear sirens," said Casey. "I'll bring them around back."

"Thanks, sugar."

Casey returned with two uniformed police officers. "There he is. He's trying to get into Madam LeJeune's property again."

"He was arrested yesterday for breaking in," said Misty. "He's on bail, and now I'll have to press more charges against him."

"Is he a stalker?" asked one of the officers.

"If a stalker is someone who watches my house and follows me around, I'd say yes."

The cop reached down to give Linc a hand out of the fishpond, but he shook his head. "No, I don't want to come out. I want to swim all day."

"It's January, buddy. You really are nuts."

Both officers pulled on Linc, and he wouldn't come out of the water. "What the hell is wrong with this guy?"

"You're soaking wet and it's cold out. Let's go."

Misty released the spell as the officers made one final heave. Linc launched out of the water, and started to run. He ran through the gate and down the back lane towards the street. "She tried to drown me. Misty LeJeune is an evil witch, and she tried to drown me."

The one officer shook his head. "He's a looney toon. Catch him and add resisting arrest."

Once the officers had Linc Castille secured in the back of the squad car, they came back to the house and took statements from everyone. The girls were super hyped but she pre-warned them not to mention the spell. "Rule number one: we never speak about magick to non-believers."

Casey, however, was more accustomed to the drill having lived on the streets and worked with Blaine. "Yeah, I was the one who first saw him breaking in. That's a repeat offense, right there. The judge just granted him bail this morning after breaking in yesterday and hurting Madam Claire and Madam Angelique. We've got a restraining order in the works too. That dude should be in jail."

The officer nodded and put away his notebook. "I'm sure he won't be so lenient tomorrow morning. Good afternoon."

Algiers Point

Claire was a well-trained and disciplined psychic who usually gave summer classes at Lily Dale, the psychic community in New York State. She slowly walked through the home of Jules Ireland and observed his lifestyle both visually and spiritually. The townhome was upscale—granite countertops, stainless steel appliances, and a restaurant-style gourmet stove with six burners. After covering the main floor, Claire ventured upstairs and began in the master suite. She touched different items on the victim's dresser and didn't feel much energy emanating from any of them.

"Your daughter got the strongest result from the first victim's closet," said Lieutenant White. "Maybe try there."

Claire entered the closet and began touching the neatly hung suits. There was a strong aroma of perfume coming from a charcoal gray suit at the end of the rack.

What's that scent? I recognize it.

"What is it?" Lieutenant White asked.

Claire didn't care for interruptions. Fragments of images flashed through Claire's mind, and she focused on sorting them. "There's something in the mail we need to look at."

Luke turned to Lieutenant White. "Is there any unopened mail downstairs?"

"Let's go check." The lieutenant jogged down the staircase ahead of them. "Forensics printed everything here, but they may have returned it by now."

Luke waited for Claire at the bottom of the stairs and then followed White down to the front hall and then into the dining room. "Here's the victim's returned property."

Luke put on a pair of latex gloves and looked through the bills and letters that were already open and in the evidence bag. "Nothing here sticks out to me."

"Perhaps in the box, newly delivered," Claire suggested.

The lieutenant took a small mailbox key off the hook by the door and read the tag. "Box three, slot seven."

She and Luke waited on the front porch as he walked the two houses down and across the street. A moment later, he was returning with a smile on his face. "Look what I have here. It's the receipt for an engagement ring from the same jewelry store as the first victim."

Luke raised his auburn brows. "Somebody doesn't want these guys getting married."

Lieutenant White put the key back on the hook and locked up. "We'll take another look at the jewelry store personnel and see if we can link the third victim. Thank you so much for your help, Madam."

"You're welcome, Lieutenant. I hope you find her."

White cranked his head around. "Pardon, Madam? Did you see that the killer is a woman?"

"No, but her perfume is lingering on one of the victim's suits upstairs in the closet. The charcoal gray one at the end of the rack."

White had his notebook in his hand. "Did you recognize the scent or the brand?"

"I believe its Chanel, but can't be sure which fragrance. Perhaps you could have the suit analyzed?"

"Of course, I can." He smiled. "Thank you so much, Madam Le Jeune. You've been extremely helpful."

CHAPTER FIFTEEN

Saturday, January 14th.

<u>Nine Saint Gillian Street</u>

Luke joined Casey outside on the back porch for a smoke. The air was cool and crisp, but the sun shone brightly, and the day promised to warm up later. He'd always liked Casey. He was a good kid dealt a tough life. A diamond in the rough, sort of boy. "No school today, Casey. You have plans?"

He exhaled a cloud of smoke and shrugged. "Don't have any friends here in New Orleans. The only people I know are you and Misty."

"And three pretty girls. One of them appeal to you?"

He shrugged again. "Michele is the prettiest, but she doesn't like me. She and Charlotte are way older than me anyway. Diana likes me, but she's shy."

"Nothing wrong with shy. Shy can be nice."

He tilted his head as if considering that. "Okay, maybe not right now. You could take a walk down the street and get to know the neighborhood. You might run into someone your age and strike up a conversation."

Casey looked like he was about to reply when he turned his head. "Do you hear a cat?"

The two of them stepped off the back deck and walked across the grass to peer down the lane. Linc Castille was running towards them with a big black cat under his arm.

Luke cursed. "You get on out of here, Linc. I'll arrest you again if you set foot on this property."

The guy held up the cat and started shouting out what could have been a spell. It was hard to tell; he wasn't making much sense.

Casey reached to his back pocket and scowled. "Damn it. I don't have my wand."

"I don't need one," Misty snapped, as she ran past them and across the garden.

Stars and moon come aid my plight
Help make this Linc problem right
Sleep all day and sleep all night
So mote it be

Linc Castille laid down at the side of the laneway, closed his eyes, and went to sleep. The big black cat ran off, and Misty looked to them, her beautiful face muddled with confusion.

"Don't look at me," he said. "That guy is off his rocker. I'll call the police and have him picked up."

"Again," Casey offered.

"Again," he and Misty repeated.

"Do you think the sleep spell was too harsh?" asked Misty.

"Just right," said Casey. "Wish I could cast a spell like that, and have it work."

"Soon, sweetheart. It takes a lot of practice. Daddy made me practice for hours when I wanted to go out and play with my friends."

"But look at all you can do now. You are the queen."

Misty giggled. "Flattery will get you banana pancakes for breakfast. Let's go in."

Casey headed inside, and Misty took Luke's hand and held him back a little.

Luke leaned in, and his heart started tripping in his chest. "Everything okay?"

She nodded. "I just wanted to say thanks for this week. You've been a rock, and I'm so grateful to have you here."

He was about to say it was no problem when she gripped his jaw and kissed him. And damn, did she ever kiss him. She moved her mouth over his and pressed her body tight against his like she meant it.

He wrapped his arms around her and took what she gave him. Misty was a beautifully made female, with curves and dips in all the right places. He tried to keep from getting handsy, but it was tough.

His hand gripped the round of her ass as she ground against him. He tried not to overstep but wanted to show her that yeah, he was interested too.

When she eased back, they were both breathless.

Misty giggled and brushed her fingers over her lips. "I hope you don't mind. I've wanted to do that for a while now."

Luke was dumbstruck. "Not a bit. I'm glad you let me know. I've uh, been thinking along those lines too."

"Along those lines?" Misty said, biting her bottom lip. "What were you thinking?"

Luke felt his cheeks flush warm. "Well, that might not be appropriate considering that we just had our first kiss."

Misty's eyes lit up with a mischief he was growing to love. "Oh, now I definitely want to know. Let's explore that thought and have some fun together later today."

Luke smiled, his body fueled with a hunger he hadn't felt in years. "It's a date. And I gotta say, I'm looking forward to getting you alone."

Misty giggled. "Not half as much as I am."

Angelique placed a big stack of pancakes in the center of the dining room table, and everyone dug in to eat. That's when the knock came on the back door to go outside to deal with the police. "I'll go," Luke said.

"Your breakfast is going to get cold," Misty protested.

"I make more later," said Angelique.

"I'll go out too, in case Luke has trouble explaining about Linc and why he's sleeping."

Casey pushed back his chair, and Claire laid a hand on his arm. "Let them handle it, dear. Eat your breakfast. They'll be right back."

Misty scruffed Casey's dark hair as she rounded the table. "I promise to call if we need you, buddy."

By the time Misty joined the conversation, the uniformed officers were already staring down at Linc snoring away in the back lane. "Is this guy a hobo?"

"No," said Luke. "He has his own security company, but he's been stalking Madam LeJeune and trespassing on her property. He's been arrested two or three times before."

"So… now he sleeps in the back lane of her house?" asked the other officer.

Luke shrugged with a bit of a smirk on his face. "I guess he's tired. Honestly, I don't think the guy is all there."

The officer gave him a couple of nudges, but Linc was out cold. "Okay, we'll give him a bunk until tomorrow."

Luke and Misty went back inside to finish breakfast, and Angelique had made a fresh batch of pancakes. Casey had finished breakfast and was sitting at the end of the table with Linc Castille's big black cat purring happily on his lap.

"Where'd he come from?" Misty asked.

"He ran in as you walked out," Casey said. "And he

seems to like me."

"How could he know? Do you think he's Linc's cat, or did he grab him in the back lane?"

Casey shrugged. "Hard to guess. There's been a lot of weird stuff happening around that guy."

Luke flooded his pancakes with syrup. "Linc couldn't take a cat to jail even if he is his. You're doing him a favor."

Misty made a face. "He didn't do me any favors."

"What should we call him?" asked Casey.

Misty's mother set her coffee mug onto the table. "Perhaps he already has a name, son. Why don't you ask him."

Casey grinned. "Like he will tell me?"

"No, but I might catch his thoughts."

Casey's eyes widened. He bent his head lower and asked, "What's your name, kitty?"

Everyone was quiet while she concentrated. "Walter," said Claire. "His name is Walter."

"Mother, cats aren't named Walter."

Claire shrugged. "I'm sure he knows his own name."

Angelique laughed. "I call him *Kitty*. Walter is a bad name."

"I had a friend named Walter," said Josiah. "He passed himself off as a wizard, but he was only a stage magician."

Her mother broke into a devilish grin. "I remember

him. Quite an attractive man."

Josiah huffed. "That's why I never took my eyes off you when he was around, my love. My wand was at the ready to turn him into a white rabbit."

Her mother laughed. "Oh, Josiah. No one ever held a candle to you, darling."

"Didn't we have a black cat when I was little, Daddy?"

"We did. What was her name, my love?"

"That was too long ago for me to remember. Maybe it was Salem. When we were first married, you named every familiar you had Salem."

"Rubbish. I did not."

Her mother laughed. "Yes, you did."

An hour after they'd cleared the breakfast dishes, there was a tremendous banging on the front door. Misty left her Tarot cards spread out in the parlor and headed for the foyer. Luke jogged down the stairs and held up a hand. "Stay there, Misty. I'll see who it is."

While Luke opened the door, Misty stood back to look at the man standing on the front porch. Surprisingly enough, he looked a lot like Linc Castille. "I'm Jefferson Castille, and I've just come from the city jail. My brother can't wake up, and I know Madam LeJeune has cast a spell on him."

"And why are you here, sir?" asked Luke politely.

"I want the spell removed from my brother."

Misty entered the front hall, stood next to Luke. "The spell will end when I'm convinced Linc will stop trying to break into my house to steal from me."

"So, you admit you have him under a sleep spell?"

"Of course. He was warned more than once to stay away from this house."

"I'm going to the police to have you charged, Madam LeJeune," Jefferson said.

"With what? Using a self-defense magick spell against a robber? Good luck with that."

"I'll make them listen." He turned around and stormed down the flagstone walkway to his truck.

Luke closed the door and sighed. "Time to change all the codes again. If he's involved too, he might know what Linc did to the panel of the security system.

"Should we talk to their mother again?" asked Misty. "She seemed like the most reasonable of the three."

"Maybe."

Casey had been lurking in the hallway listening to the conversation at the front door. "If we go down to Houma, we could check on Wannabe at Luke's gran's house."

Angelique shook her long dark hair. "He lives in de swamp now. I never want d'at slimy *grenouille* back here."

"Don't worry, *ma chere*. I'm not bringing him back."

Luke shrugged. "Well, if we did go, I could check

on my grandmother, and pick up my wand and a few things I have in a box under my bed."

"Ooh, you have a wand? I want to see your kit, Lukey. Let's go for a drive."

***

Houma, Louisiana

As Luke drove down to Houma, memories of growing up with his grandmother came back to him. Well-respected for her powers and knowledge in her day, she taught him everything she knew. When he went into the police academy right after high school, he left his powers behind in the bayou.

Checking that Casey had his earbuds in, and he could talk privately, he took Misty's hand as he drove. "I never talk about it, but when my daughter was born, I hoped she'd have some of my powers. I didn't have the chance to find out. She was barely two when she was killed in the accident with my wife."

Misty's green eyes welled up with tears. "I'm so sorry, Luke. How terrible for you."

"I'm better now than I was, and better now that I'm back home in N'Orlean with you. But, I gotta be honest with you, Misty. Part of my heart will always belong to them. I don't want to hurt you, but if we're going to go beyond that kiss this morning, you should know what you're getting into."

Misty squeezed his fingers and turned in her seat to face him. "Aw, sugar, I get that. Then, if this is true confessions, you should know that part of my heart will always belong to Blaine. Blacky and I come from different worlds, and neither of us is willing to give up that part of ourselves. We said our goodbyes and accept that we are over, but that doesn't erase those feelings from my heart. I still have plenty of love to give, though."

The rest of the drive was pretty quiet. Luke knew Misty and Blaine loved each other, and if she was willing to move forward, he'd do the same.

A second chance for both of them.

When they arrived at Madam Castille's house, there was no one home. Luke knocked three times, and went around back, but there was no answer.

"Maybe she saw us pull up and doesn't want another confrontation," said Misty.

Luke didn't think so. "No vehicle in the driveway this time. She could be out shopping. We'll try back on our way home."

Bayou Country, Louisiana

Madam Hyslop was home when they arrived at her little house at the edge of the bayou, but Misty was sad to see that she'd fallen ill since their last visit. She was resting in bed, wrapped in a shawl, when they got there, but looked terribly pale.

"I'm worried, Misty. I can't leave her here alone."

"We'll take her home with us. There are plenty of extra guest rooms on the second floor, and Angelique will be delighted to care for her while she's on the mend."

"Gran," said Luke. "Misty and I want to take you home to N'Orlean until you're feeling better. Will you come?"

"I don't want to be a bother, dear."

"Misty has a gifted lady who will take care of you. A bayou woman, like you."

"You're no bother, Madam Hyslop," Misty said, offering her a warm smile. "Do you have a bag we could put some of your clothes in?"

"In the closet."

Luke moved to help, and Misty waved him off. "I'll do it, sugar. You take care of your Gran."

"I'll check on Wannabe," Casey said, retreating outside.

Misty packed an overnight bag with clothes and essentials but worried that Madam Hyslop might not be comfortable traveling for an hour in her condition.

"I'll grab my stuff from under my bed, and then we'll be off, okay, Gran?" He returned from his bedroom a moment later, carrying a dusty cardboard box full of his belongings.

Misty sat Madam Hyslop up and sat next to her. "Luke, why don't you fix the seats in the truck so your grandmother can lie down on the trip home."

"Good idea. I'll be right back."

Once the truck was ready, Misty grabbed two pillows and a couple of blankets and walked out behind them. Luke was a big, strong man, and his grandmother looked even frailer in his arms.

Once she was settled in the back seat, Misty glanced around for Casey. "Casey, where are you? We're leaving now."

He came running through the trees from the edge of the river. "I don't see Wannabe, but I saw a couple of gators sunning themselves on the far bank. I bet they ate him."

Misty giggled. "They wouldn't eat a slimy frog."

Luke raised an eyebrow. "I think they might."

"I'm not telling the girls that story, and Casey, you better not either. You'll cause a torrent of tears."

Casey chuckled.

Nine Saint Gillian Street

Angelique was thrilled to have Luke's grandmother to care for. She made her comfortable in one of the guest rooms on the second floor, then fixed her a tray of hot soup, cornbread, and restorative Oolong tea.

Luke spent a few minutes with her before he went down to dinner. "You'll feel better soon, Gran. When you're ready, I'll take you home, but I want you to stay with us as long as you want to. I'm uneasy with you living alone so far away from me and anyone who might be able to check on you."

His grandmother smiled. "I'm glad you've come back to me, Lukey. I can see how happy you are spending time with Madam LeJeune. She is a good one for you. I see good things ahead for the two of you."

"I am happy, Gran. Happy for the first time in a long time."

After everyone in the house had gone to bed, Misty let Hoo out for a run, then she locked the doors and set the alarm. In her room, she changed into her favorite yellow nightie, brushed the lengths of her hair, then tiptoed next door to Luke's room.

His door was open a crack, and his big, beautiful body was stretched out under the covers while he relaxed and read a book. A flutter of anxiety tickled her belly when she pushed the door open a little wider.

The moment his eyes locked on her, she knew she was welcome. He put the book on the bedside table and pulled back the blankets.

She closed them in together, slid under the covers, and cuddled up to his warm muscular body. "I came to wish you a good night."

Luke chuckled and pulled her into his arms, his hands already tracing her curves. "Forget good night. This just turned into a *great* night."

CHAPTER SIXTEEN

Sunday, January 15th.

<u>Nine Saint Gillian Street</u>

Luke smoked on the back porch reliving the pleasures of the night before with Misty in his bed. A powerhouse of energy, she had worn him out, and he'd slept later than he usually did. His stomach growled, and he smiled. He'd also worked up one hell of an appetite. He called Hoo away from the fishpond and took the dog inside for breakfast.

"Don't chase Walter," said Luke, as they walked down the back hall to the kitchen. Hoo didn't listen, and as soon as he saw the big black furball, the Bernese was on the run. "Casey, save the cat."

Casey ran towards the front parlor and grabbed the cat up off the floor before Hoo nabbed him. "Got you, Walter. Wait until the girls see you tomorrow."

Luke cleaned his plate, sure that no bacon omelet had ever tasted as good. It could have had something to do with the blonde across the table, though. Misty took his breath away.

They'd barely finished the last of their breakfast when the doorbell rang and set off another round of Hoo barking and running in circles. "You expecting anyone?" he asked, Misty.

"No. My client isn't coming until this afternoon."

"Let me get it then. Hang back a bit until we see who it is." He pushed out of his chair and headed down the hall. He opened the door to Madam Castille, who pushed herself into the foyer.

"I wish to speak to Madam LeJeune."

Misty strode down the hall and lifted her chin. "What is it, Madam?"

"Jefferson is certain you cast a spell on Lincoln. I'd like you to remove it."

"I'd like your son to stop breaking into my home to steal my family book. You and Jefferson gave me the impression that will never happen, so it follows the spell won't be removed. I feel the truth of your magick, Madam. If you want the spell removed, figure it out, yourself."

The black cat ran through the foyer and down the hall with Hoo after it. "That was Walter," said Madam Castille. "You've stolen Lincoln's familiar?"

Misty rolled her eyes. "He was alone in the back lane after they took Linc to jail. I've been taking care of Walter."

"I doubt that. I'll take him home now." She grabbed Walter, and as she lifted him, he clawed her face. A red gash drew blood under her right eye, and she let off an awful screech. She pointed a bony finger at Walter.

> *Misbehaved and spoiled brat*
> *I curse you, you stupid ca—*

Misty whipped out her wand to counter.

> *Spell that's cast will not last*
> *Spell diminish*
> *Do not finish*
> *Reverso*

The two spells collided in a huge puff of pink smoke. Madam Castille's eyes grew furious, and then she stormed out the front door.

Luke closed and locked the door behind her.

Angelique clapped her hands. "How did you manage d'at pink smoke, Madam?"

"Yeah, that was so cool," Casey added.

Misty shrugged. "I'm not sure. It just happened."

Casey leaned down and picked up the black cat. "And we still have Walter. Maybe he's ours to keep now."

Claire strode down the stairs, a frown marring her face. "I wouldn't count on it, son. The Castilles don't seem like givers. More like takers."

At two o'clock, Luke opened the door and welcomed

Misty's client. He'd decided not to let the women in the household answer the door anymore while he was on the premises. Too much was going on, and he wanted to screen the callers to be on the safe side. "Good afternoon, Miss Teatro. Please, follow me into the parlor."

The woman, who was shorter than average and on the opposite end of the spectrum from pretty, was dressed in a black business suit and black pumps. She glanced around the foyer and down the hallways as if she knew Misty's reputation and was expecting to see some amazing witchy things in every corner. Luke escorted her straight into the front parlor.

Claire walked past the doorway and stopped, looking puzzled. She tilted her head for him to come into the hall, and he nodded. As soon as Miss Teatro was seated at the Tarot reading table with Misty, he joined her.

"What is it, Claire?"

Misty's mother leaned close to his ear and whispered. "She's wearing the same Chanel perfume that was on the suit of the second victim."

Luke raised an eyebrow. Chanel was a popular fragrance, so that didn't necessarily mean anything, but still, the way things had been going for them lately, what were the odds of that? "I'll keep an eye on her."

Misty began the reading the way she always did, by getting a feel for a new client. "Tell me a bit about what brought you here, Miss Teatro. Do you have a question to ask? Perhaps a decision weighing on you? How can I help you this afternoon?"

"Umm… well, I live alone, well not totally alone, I have a bird who keeps me company. A talking budgie named Pudgy. He's extremely intelligent."

Walter strutted through the room, the fur on the back of his neck standing up in a ruff. He stopped next to Misty's chair and stared up at Miss Teatro.

Meow

"Oh, what a lovely cat." She stuck her hand down to stroke his head, and Walter bared his teeth and hissed."

"Bad kitty," she scolded. "Madam LeJeune, perhaps you shouldn't have your cat near your guests."

Misty shrugged. "It's not my cat. Walter's a visitor in my home. He's free to roam and to have an opinion."

Angelique entered with a tray. "Tea, Madam?"

"Thank you, *chere*." Misty shuffled the cards, while Miss Teatro accepted some of Angelique's peppermint tea. When she was all set, she passed her the deck to shuffle. "Shuffle until you feel comfortable, then stop and cut the deck."

By the way the woman held the cards, she'd never shuffled a deck in her life. "How do you come to be here today?"

"I heard about you, Madam LeJeune, and what you do. I thought it might be interesting to meet you."

Misty smiled and took the cards back, shuffling them herself. "And where did you hear my name mentioned?"

"Oh, here and there. You've got a reputation."

Misty glanced across the room at Luke flipping through a magazine. He looked totally absorbed, but she knew he was listening to every word of the conversation.

"Well, without a question or any direction to give, let's see what the cards have to say, shall we? Please choose a card and set in front of you. Then choose two more and set them to either side of the first."

Misty waited until the woman followed her instruction and then flipped the first card face up. "This is your Significator card, Miss Teatro."

"If you say so."

"Knight of cups in shadow suggests something unseen. A secret kept or something done that you don't want people to know about. Does that resonate with you in any way?"

"No, of course not. What are you implying?"

"Nothing. The Tarot is simply pointing something out."

"Ridiculous." Miss Teatro's hands were shaking, to the point that she placed them in her lap.

"Alright, let's see what the next card says?" Misty flipped the second card. "This is the Devil card, also in shadow."

"I don't believe in the Devil."

"The Devil card has little to nothing to do with modern conceptions of evil, Miss Teatro. Tarot doesn't work like that."

Her client stood up and reached for her jacket on the

back of her chair. "Enough of this, Madam LeJeune. You're trying to scare me."

Misty said nothing. Disturbing vibes were shooting off the woman, like poison darts. The aura around her head was dark and murderous.

Luke saw Miss Teatro to the door, locked it, and returned to the front parlor. "What was that about?"

"Find out if Miss Teatro works at the jewelry store, Lukey. If she does, she might well be the one Lieutenant White is looking for."

CHAPTER SEVENTEEN

Monday, January 16th.

<u>Nine Saint Gillian Street</u>

At a quarter to nine, the girls arrived for school, and Casey waited for them in the front foyer with Walter in his arms.

Diana squealed. "Ooh, a new kitty. She ran straight to Casey to pet the cat. "His fur is so soft. What's his name?"

"Walter. He told Madam LeJeune his name was Walter."

Charlotte went wide-eyed. "He told her his name?"

Claire smiled. "I read his little kitty mind, dear. I asked him his name, and when he thought of it, I caught his thoughts."

"That is something I want to learn to do," said Michele. "It would help me so much when I'm reading tea leaves."

"What could tea leaves possibly tell you?" asked Casey.

"It's an older form of divination, dear," said Claire. "There are some who are extremely skilled readers."

"My grandmother is one of them," said Michele.

"Let's go upstairs and get ready for our first class, shall we?" Claire herded her tribe towards the staircase.

Once the students were out of the way, Luke spent some time with Gran in her room. "You didn't eat much breakfast, Gran."

"I ate what I could. Madam LaFontaine is a marvelous cook. She's taking such good care of me."

"Can I get you something to read?"

"Maybe this afternoon, I'll get up and sit in that chair by the window. Right now, I'm going to rest for an hour."

Luke smiled. He leaned down and kissed her cheek. "I'll close your door to keep the noise out."

He went back to his room to unpack some of his stored belongings when Hoo barked and signaled someone at the door. "I'll get it, Misty," he called out as he ran down the stairs.

"Lieutenant White. Come in." Luke glanced into the front parlor, and Angelique shook her head. She was cleansing the room of the negative energy left by Miss Teatro. "Let's use the sitting room at the back of the house. I'll call Misty from the kitchen."

"I wish my wife spent half the time in the kitchen that Madam LeJeune does." He gave a little chuckle.

Misty joined them moments later and sat down on

the gray leather loveseat next to Luke. "We had a visitor yesterday, Lieutenant."

"So, I understand. Did you pick up anything useful?"

"It's all useful, isn't it?" asked Misty.

"Yes, of course. Even with the help you've given us, we haven't nailed down a viable suspect. Everyone who was re-interviewed had a solid alibi."

"Was Babette Teatro one of those interviewed?"

Lieutenant White shook his head. "She isn't on the list."

"When she was here yesterday, Mother said Miss Teatro wore the same perfume that lingered on the suit in victim number two's closet. It might be a coincidence, but I don't believe it is. With the dark energy coming off her and what the cards were trying to say, I'd bet she's involved."

Lieutenant White nodded. "We need evidence. I can't arrest someone based on your gifts, no matter how much I respect them. Before I bring Miss Teatro in for questioning would you consider going to the residence of the third victim?"

Luke shook his head. "Not a good idea for Misty."

"Perhaps if Madam LeJeune Senior went also?" asked White. "It might not be such a burden on Madam Misty if her mother was there."

"Claire is teaching today," Luke said.

"Perhaps we could go over tonight?" Misty offered.

Lieutenant White looked relieved. "I'll arrange to

meet you there at seven. Does that work for y'all?"

"I'm sure it'll be fine. You can send Luke the address."

***

Holy Cross Area, New Orleans

John Ritchie's home—a two-storey townhouse with a for sale sign on the lawn—was one unit in a long row of identical-looking units. Lieutenant White held the door for the LeJeune ladies and then followed them inside the house. The foyer was small, all the furniture still in place the same way Mr. Ritchie had left it. "Where would the ladies like to start?"

Misty looked at her mother. "I prefer to start in the bedroom. It's the most personal for the deceased and usually gives off the strongest energy."

"That's fine with me, darling. How long has Mr. Ritchie been deceased, Lieutenant?"

"Six weeks now, Madam."

The second floor smelled a little musty and closed up, but there was a hint of something else on the air, perhaps cologne or aftershave. Misty found herself being drawn toward the ensuite and decided to check the medicine cabinet.

White walked close behind her with his notebook in hand.

Misty stared at her reflection in the vanity mirror, then reached for the knob on the medicine chest hanging above the toilet. As the door swung open, negative energy rushed out of the medicine chest like a choking

SCHOOL FOR RELUCTANT WITCHES · 213

cloud of evil.

Misty stumbled back as the room spun.

Lieutenant White, only a couple of feet away, rushed to catch her before she fainted.

"It's in there. What you need."

Luke rushed in and took care of Misty, while Lieutenant White removed every item from the medicine cabinet and placed it on the granite surface of the vanity.

Misty sat on the side of the tub with her head in her hands. She glanced up and pointed. "The one with the gift tag."

Luke leaned forward. "To John, with love. Babs."

"Babette Teatro," Misty said. "There's your connection to the third victim."

"Amazing, Madam. Truly amazing."

Luke helped Misty up and supported her as they walked into the master suite. Her mother was busy touching items of clothing in the closet. "Anything, Mother?"

"Nothing in the closet except the same Chanel fragrance lingering on two of his suits."

"I'll have Miss Teatro brought in for questioning," said Lieutenant White. "You ladies have my deepest gratitude."

CHAPTER EIGHTEEN

Tuesday, January 17th.

<u>Nine Saint Gillian Street</u>

The minute Luke was showered and dressed, he tapped on the door of the room next to his to check on his grandmother. Alarmed by the paleness and translucency of her skin, he spoke to her in a soft whisper. "Gran, are you all right?"

She opened her eyes and looked at him with a smile on her lips. "I'm tired this morning, Lukey."

"I'll make you tea. What would you like for breakfast?"

"I'm not hungry, but tea would be wonderful."

Luke raced downstairs to the kitchen. "Gran is fading. Is there anything we can do?"

Misty squeezed his hand and offered him a smile. "The kids can help me. We can do a healing spell."

Luke didn't doubt Misty's powers, but some things were beyond the realm of her control. "She's asking for tea."

"I'll bring a cup," said Angelique.

Upstairs in his Gran's room, Angelique methodically went about lighting blue candles to enhance the healing spell.

Misty assembled a basket of fruits and vegetables as a gift to the goddess and was about to climb the stairs when Hoo barked, and the girls arrived. "Casey, hang up their coats, then y'all come to Gran's room. We need all the positive energy we can get for the healing spell."

"We'll be right there, Misty."

"Is Luke's Gran worse?" asked Diana.

"Yes. We have to help her," said Casey. "Hurry."

Claire hustled the students into the bedroom and told them where to stand. "Now hold hands around the bed while Misty says the spell."

On every surface, blue candles burned, and the room filled with fragrance. Luke's Gran lay pale on her bed.

"Everyone focus good thoughts for Luke's Gran while I invoke the spell," said Misty. She raised her hands and focused her green eyes on the ceiling of the room.

> *Goddess of the stars and moon*
> *Grant my plea and make it soon*
> *Heal Luke's Gran and grant her health*
> *She has no strength*
> *She has no wealth*
> *Make her strong to face the day*
> *Accept our thanks and our gifts, we pray*
> *So mote it be*

Misty chanted the incantation three times, then held the basket of gifts above her head as an offering to the goddess.

Luke stayed with her all morning. Shortly before lunch, his grandmother's eyes flickered open. He reached over and squeezed her hand. "Hey, there. Do you feel better, Gran?"

She smiled at him, and he'd never felt such a wave of relief wash through him. "I do."

"Could I get you some lunch?"

"Thank you, yes. I'd like some soup if they have it. And if it's not too much trouble, perhaps a roll or some bread?"

Luke raised his eyes to the heavens and thanked the goddess, then sent his thanks to the rest of them. Rising up, he leaned over the bed and kissed Gran's forehead. "I love you."

"I love you, too, dear."

After asking Angelique to prepare Gran some soup, he went to the dining room to get the tray. He happened to glance through the sidelight next to the front door and recognized Detective Ellis's car parked at the curb in front of number nine Saint Gillian. Strolling down the flagstone walk, he opened the iron gate, leaned into the passenger window. "What are you doing here, Detective?"

"I'm off work with a broken foot. I'm perfectly

within my rights to sit in my car in a public place."

"Misty was in the house when you fell. I know you blame her, but—"

"She *made* it happen," he snapped. "That woman is evil."

"She's not evil. And you don't believe in magick. You said that more than once."

Ellis scowled at him. "Something is going on. She might have everyone else fooled, but I'll expose her evil ways."

Luke bristled. "Madam LeJeune helps more people in a day than you have in your entire lifetime."

"She'll make a mistake, and then I'll arrest her," said Ellis. "It won't be long."

Before he did something he *wouldn't* regret, Luke went inside and locked the door. He set the alarm and was about to head upstairs to check on Gran when his cell rang. "Yeah, Luke Hyslop."

"Afternoon, Ranger Hyslop, this is Lieutenant White. I wanted to thank you and the ladies again for your help. Miss Teatro has been brought in for questioning. While she isn't an employee of the jewelry shop, she is an insurance appraiser they brought in for higher-priced items. I'm sure we'll be able to connect the dots from there."

"I'm glad you're happy, Lieutenant. If I may, there's something I want to bring to your attention."

"Oh, what is it?"

"Detective Ellis is parked in front of Madam

LeJeune's house and says he plans to stay there until he can arrest her."

"For what?"

"Apparently for her inherent evil. I'd appreciate it if you had a word with him. If his crusade persists, sir, we'll be filing harassment charges, and don't be surprised to find the LeJeunes far less welcoming in the future."

"Please extend my apologies to the ladies. I'll take care of it, Mr. Hyslop, you have my word on that, sir."

Misty had an appointment at one o'clock to give a new client a reading. Her mother had asked if the students could sit in the front parlor and observe Misty's techniques.

Before the guest arrived, her mother got them all seated and settled. Walter jumped into Casey's lap and started to purr. "Now, all of you," she said. "Sit quietly and not a word. You're here to observe only. Promise me."

"We promise."

At precisely one on the dot, the doorbell rang. Luke greeted the client and brought her into the parlor. "Good afternoon. I'm Mystere LeJeune."

"Bridget Wraight, Madam." She offered her hand. "I'm excited to meet you."

"Please come in, Miss Wraight. Take a seat. "I have several students on hand today. They are here to observe me, not you, so pay no attention to them. Pretend they're not here."

"Students? You give lessons?"

"Not really, no. They just happened. Shall we begin?"

Misty took the Tarot deck out of the velvet bag and began shuffling the cards. She watched the client, and the client watched her.

Suddenly, Walter vaulted from Casey's lap and landed squarely in the middle of the table. Miss Wraight screamed and leaned back. Walter hissed, and Casey scooped the angry cat off the table.

"I've changed my mind," said Miss Wraight. "This is a mistake. I want to leave. Would you get my coat?"

"Of course," said Misty. She walked across the foyer and noticed Luke standing across the hall in the doorway to the dining room observing.

"Another client storms out? Reminds me of Miss Teatro."

Misty brushed her hair from her face and exhaled. "Similar vibes too. Connected, maybe?"

Luke pushed off and headed for the stairs. "Let me check the two names on my computer. I'll be back in a minute."

Misty sat at the table and blew out a long breath.

"Sorry, Misty," Casey said. "Walter hated that woman. I couldn't hold him."

"Perhaps he had good reason," said Josiah. "My familiars always knew a good person from a bad one."

Luke came bounding down the stairs with a slip of paper in his hand. "The lady who just left was Miss Teatro's sister."

Misty's green eyes widened. "Her sister? What does she want with us? We don't know anything about the murders her sister committed other than what Lieutenant White told us, and we don't want to know."

"Maybe she was on a fishing expedition," said Luke. "I'm phoning Lieutenant White."

He walked across the hall into the dining room to talk where it was quiet, and Misty followed him. "Miss Teatro's sister came here today, pretending to want a reading. How did she know about Misty? You vowed to keep her out of the case."

Luke covered the microphone of the cell and shook his head. "He swears he never told anyone about you or your mother helping him."

"Did Miss Teatro have a visitor in jail?" Misty wondered.

Luke relayed the question and shook his head. "Not that he knows of, but will check with lockup and get back to us."

Luke ended the call, and she could tell he was upset. She pulled him into a hug and stroked the back of his long auburn hair. "Don't worry, sugar. The case is all but wrapped up. We don't have to bother with it anymore."

Ten minutes passed before Lieutenant White called back. "No one came to see Miss Teatro except her attorney. No other visitors."

"Uh-huh." Luke wasn't convinced.

"Seeing as how y'all are already upset, this is probably a bad time to ask Madam to help me find a missing girl."

"It certainly is," said Luke. "The police department can't keep Misty's name out of things, so I'm sorry, she'll have to decline, sir."

"Help with what?" Claire asked. "What's the case?"

"A missing girl."

"I'll do it. Tell him to bring a picture of the child and clothing, a toy, whatever the parents can provide."

Luke frowned. "Are you sure?"

"Quite sure, dear. I'll deal with whatever comes my way, and protect my daughter from those who want to harm her."

"Bravo, darling," said Josiah. He'd taken to following his wife from room to room.

Claire herded the students to the third floor. "Let's finish our Tarot practice upstairs. We may have another interruption when Lieutenant White comes."

"Can we watch when you try to find the little girl?" asked Charlotte.

"I suppose so. An audience has never bothered me."

Misty smiled. Her mother loved the limelight. The exact opposite of her.

Upstairs in the classroom, Claire continued with their

Tarot lesson. "Tomorrow will be our first test day. Each one of you will give me a reading on cards I pull from the deck, and I'll grade you according to accuracy, intuition, and understanding. I suggest you study your notes tonight because you won't be allowed to use them."

"What if we fail the test?" Diana asked, looking panicked.

"If you fail, you fail," said Claire. "Back to studying. But, the test will reveal where your weaknesses are, and we can concentrate on filling in the gaps of your knowledge."

Charlotte nodded. "That's good, Madam. I want to know where my strengths and weaknesses lie. A test is a good idea."

Misty called from the bottom of the stairs, "Mother, Lieutenant White is here."

"We'll be right down, dear. Thank you."

"Now, my young witches, let's see if we can find a lost little girl."

Misty and Luke sat with Lieutenant White in the front parlor. He'd brought a bag of items given to him by the child's parents. "Let Mother select what she wants to work with," said Misty.

"I have no right to ask this, Madam LeJeune, but if your mother is not successful, would you try? I know how gifted you are and the accuracy of your visions."

Misty appreciated the man's confidence in her but

didn't think her help would be necessary. "Mother is on the case. She is an expert in the field."

Her mother entered the room, her entourage following closely on her heels. The minute Casey sat down in one of the wing chairs, Walter jumped onto his lap and began purring.

"He likes you," Diana said. "The cat has good taste."

Casey smiled, and Misty winked at him.

Her mother pulled the first item out of the bag. A little sheep covered in curly white wool. A blue-collar circled the sheep's neck, and a tiny bell dangled under his head.

"Oh, that's so cute," said Michele. "How old is the child?"

"Eight years old," said Lieutenant White. "She walked down the street to her friend's house—four houses away—and she never reached the other house."

"Oh, that's horrible," said Charlotte.

"Quiet, kids. Let's let Mother concentrate, shall we?"

The students clammed up and waited, watching Claire hug the lamb close to her heart.

The lieutenant waited with pen and notebook in hand.

"She's gone. Far away. Van. Cream. She's not in the city."

"She's been taken out of state?" asked the Lieutenant.

Her mother opened her eyes and put the little lamb on the table. "Yes. The moment she was picked up, the van headed for the interstate."

Lieutenant White shook his head, not liking that.

"Let me try something else," she said, pulling a powder-blue sweater out of the bag. She held it in both hands and closed her eyes. "I'm sorry, I'm getting nothing from this. Maybe the child hadn't worn this lately."

"What else is in the bag?" asked Misty. "Try another toy."

"You try, dear. I'm feeling a little light-headed."

"I'll make a tray of sweets and tea," Angelique said.

Misty tugged the bag closer and pulled out a few things. She set a book, a doll, and a Barbie doll on the coffee table in front of her. While Misty picked up the book, Charlotte picked up the doll and smoothed down the wedding dress.

As she did, a mewling sound escaped from her lips. "A room. Motel room. The TV is on." She scrunched up her face. "The TV is too loud."

Misty rounded the antique table and gathered Charlotte's hands in her own. "Let the pieces of the vision come to you, Charlotte. Don't push. As it flashes through your head, notice what you're supposed to see."

"A highway marker. One of the little blue ones."

"What number was on it?"

"Three seventy-one."

Lieutenant White wrote the number down.

"Anything else?" asked Misty. "Colors, numbers, signs, sounds in the background."

"I see an eight. A big lit up eight, but I don't know what it means."

Luke nodded. "Check to see if there's a Super Eight anywhere close to the three-seventy-one-mile marker at either end of the state, Lieutenant. It's worth a try."

"It is. Let me make a couple of calls."

CHAPTER NINETEEN

Wednesday, January 18th.

Nine Saint Gillian Street

Misty woke up next to Luke's warm body and cuddled into him. He groaned, his arms coming around her, his hips pressing his morning intentions hard against her backside. She giggled and wriggled against him. "It's so much more fun sleeping in your room than sleeping in mine."

"More fun for me, too," Luke said, his voice heavy with sleep. His hand slid to cover her breast as he started kissing her bare shoulder. "I'm falling hard and fast for you, Misty LeJeune. I might even be addicted to you."

Misty stole a glance at the clock on the nightstand. "It's still early. Maybe you'd like to indulge in that addiction once or twice more before we begin our day."

Luke chuckled. "No doubt about it."

The three girls arrived early for class and ran straight up to the third floor to do last-minute studying before their test on the Tarot. Claire hadn't finished her tea, and Casey was still eating breakfast.

"Wow, they looked serious," Casey said, finishing his juice. "Maybe I should have studied more. I don't want to look like a moron in front of the girls."

Misty walked around the table and stroked his dark hair. "You could never be a moron, sweetheart. You are gifted. I'm sure you'll give Mother a stellar reading, and if not, you will next time. I certainly didn't excel two weeks after I began. Don't put too much pressure on yourself."

"I know the Major Arcana better than I know the suits," said Casey, "but I'll give it my best shot."

"Would it make you nervous if I came up to listen in? I'd like to take notes on what I think y'all should brush up on."

Casey shrugged. "It's okay with me."

"Please do," Mother said. "That would be helpful."

"Let me freshen up my tea, and I'll be right up."

"Where's Walter?" asked Casey. "I haven't seen him since I got out of bed."

Upstairs in the classroom, the girls sat in their regular spots, and Casey sat next to Diana like he always did. He sat as far away from Michele as possible. They were at odds, and he didn't like the negative energy she was still throwing at him.

Claire sat down across the table from the students with her notebook and pen. "I wrote numbers on four pieces of paper to see who would go first, second, etcetera." She tossed the four folded pieces of paper into the center of the table. "Go ahead and take a number."

"I'm scared," said Diana. "What if I'm first?"

Casey grabbed a number and unfolded it. "You're safe. I'm first. Let's rock on, Madam Claire."

Claire picked up the deck and shuffled. She cut the deck with her non-dominant hand and turned up the top card. "Four of swords reversed."

Casey drew a deep breath and let his energy come to the fore. "Okay, four of swords in the shadow. You may be feeling strife in your life because you're fighting a lost cause. I'm sensing something you don't want to admit to yourself. This problem isn't going away, and you feel that it's throwing your life out of balance."

Claire smiled. "That was well done, Casey."

"I got the two," said Diana. "I have to go next."

"There's nothing to be nervous about, children. Say what you think the card means and relax. Quite often, you'll be correct." Claire put the four of swords back into the deck and shuffled again.

"The Emperor, in the shadow."

Diana drew a deep breath. "This is a fire element and could relate to many things. What I'm feeling at this moment is that too much rigidity could lead to a misuse of power and end in disrespect."

"Not bad, dear," said Claire. "Not bad at all." Claire glanced at Charlotte and Michele, waiting for one of them to claim number three.

"I'm third," said Charlotte."

Claire shuffled and turned up the Tower for Charlotte. "Major Arcana, dear. Do your best."

"The Tower can signify many things," said Charlotte. "A sudden upheaval, a crisis or changes in your life, but it could also be a revelation. Seeing the truth at last and ending an illusion you've been living under."

"That's your interpretation, Charlotte?" asked Claire.

"Those are the thoughts that came to me, Madam."

"Very good, Charlotte." Claire made a note.

Michele came up next. "I hope I get a happy card."

"Let's see what it is." Claire turned up the card. "Oh, four of swords again. That card wants to be heard from today. Let me get you another, Michele."

Claire put the four of swords back into the deck and reshuffled. The card she pulled the second time was the six of Pentacles. "There you go."

Michele looked at the card for a few moments. "This is a give and take card," she said. "Trading, exchanging, giving, and receiving gifts. My feeling is this card is telling us to look at both sides of the coin. Or it could be both sides of an argument. It stresses the importance of talking things over and at the same time, being a good listener."

"Wonderful, Michele. Nicely done."

Claire gave them all a reassuring smile. "I'm happy with all of your interpretations, young ones. Next week we'll go into different spreads and how to read them."

***

Luke was working at the little desk in his room when Lieutenant White called with an update on the missing girl. "Did you find her, sir?" asked Luke.

"I'm afraid not. But the information y'all provided was accurate. The man and the girl had been there at that motel. They were gone when my men arrived."

"I'm sorry to hear that. I'll let Misty, and the girls know."

Luke looked up and smiled as Misty walked into his room. He pushed back from his desk and patted his lap. She came to him with an ease that lit him up inside. "What are you going to tell me, sugar?"

He brushed his fingers behind her head and pulled her neck to his lips. "The man and the little girl were gone when the police arrived at the Super Eight."

"That's so sad," she said, swinging her fingers toward the door. When the latch clicked, he slid his hand up her shirt, and she shifted to straddle him in his seat. "We have twenty minutes before anyone misses us."

Luke stood, taking Misty with him, and strode to the bed. "Twenty minutes. I can work with that."

Misty was in the kitchen making a list of supplies she needed when the girls and Casey finished their lesson and came downstairs for a cold drink. "As soon as y'all drink your sweet tea, I want an all-out search of the house to find Walter. His food is in his dish, and he hasn't been seen since yesterday."

"Did he go outside?" asked Diana.

"No, Casey's been keeping him inside until he recognizes this as his home."

"Don't look in the basement," said a voice from the corner of the room.

"Why not, Daddy? What's down there?"

"The house likes its privacy, and I've never violated it."

Misty straightened. "You mean all these years you have never been in the basement?"

Her mother walked into the kitchen and scoffed. "I don't believe that for a minute, Josiah. You must have gone down there to fix something at one time or another."

"I have sent others down there to fix plumbing or heating, but I have never gone myself."

Misty found this fascinating. "Why, Daddy? What are you afraid of?"

"It's better not to know anything about it," he said, fading away before them.

"About what? Come back here, Daddy, and finish telling us about the basement."

Her mother rolled her eyes. "He must be teasing us. There's nothing in the basement."

Misty looked her mother in the eye. "Have you ever been down there, Mother?"

"Well, no, not exactly."

"What does that mean?"

"I've looked down the stairs a few times."

Luke shook his head. "Casey and I will go down there right now and put this to rest."

"Where's the door to the basement?" asked Casey.

"Down the hall on the left side," said Misty. "Daddy said not to go."

"I'm checking it out," said Luke. "It's silly to be afraid of the basement." Luke walked down the narrow hallway and reefed on the door. It was stuck shut. "This door hasn't been opened in ages."

"Let me loosen it up," said Casey. Before Luke could stop him, Casey kicked the old door a good one with his Harley boot. There was a loud crack, and Luke tried again.

He turned the handle, and the door squeaked as he pulled it open. Luke flicked the light switch on the wall, and no basement lights came on. "The bulbs must be burnt out if nobody ever went down there."

"We need flashlights." Casey ran back to the kitchen to get a couple.

Diana, Charlotte, and Michele followed him to the top of the stairs. "Can we come down too?"

Misty answered that one from the kitchen. "Don't go down there, girls."

Luke went first, shining the flashlight ahead of him. The room at the bottom of the stairs was empty. A cement floor, walls a foot thick around the single window, and a workbench. From there, other doors led off to the left and right. "Alright, other than a lot of cobwebs, there's nothing too spooky down here."

Luke felt a cold wind blowing from under the door to the left of where he was standing. A soft scratching was coming from the other side of the door. He pointed, and Casey nodded.

Luke frowned. "Whatever it is, it can't be human. Nobody has been down here for years."

"I'm more afraid of non-human," said Casey. "I watched *The Walking Dead* three times."

"On three, I'm going to open the door," Luke said with a grin. "You ready?"

"Not really. But go for it. I'll hold the light."

Luke counted down, turned the knob, and flung the door open. Walter ran out of the room, zoomed past both of them, and tore up the stairs.

Casey squealed a bit as the black cat tore by but collected himself quickly. "How'd he get in there? That's impossible."

Luke shrugged. "Lots of these old places have secret passages. Maybe Misty knows."

As they climbed the stairs, Casey tugged the leg of his jeans. "Hey, Luke? You won't tell the girls I lost my cool, will ya?"

Luke chuckled. "That you screeched like an eight-year-old girl? No, buddy. Your secret's safe with me."

The girls were screaming when they got back to the

kitchen. "Look at Walter. He's covered in—what is this stuff?"

"Cobwebs, dear." Claire handed them a container. "Gather them up. They're an essential ingredient in many of our everyday potions."

"In a love potion?" asked Diana.

Claire shook her head. "No. Not a love potion. Things more deadly than love."

Misty pulled one of Hoo's brushes out of a drawer and held it out. "Brush him off. He's a mess."

Casey took the brush and started the cleanup. "But how did he get down there? Walter was in a locked room behind a closed door."

"He took him," said Josiah.

Claire and Misty rolled their eyes. "He—who, Josiah? Are you making life more interesting by spinning yarns again?"

"No, my darling. I would never do that."

"Who lives in the basement, Daddy?"

"The former owner. The man who built this house way back when. George Washington Claiborne, the third."

Misty repeated the name to Luke. "Look him up and see if he ever owned this house, sugar."

Luke grinned. "Can't wait to Google him."

"So, what we're talking about is another ghost living here, yeah?" asked Casey.

Misty chuckled. "If Daddy is telling the truth."

"Why would I lie, daughter? I didn't want you to fret about old George because he's not the friendliest ghost on the planet."

Claire giggled. "Or *not* on the planet."

"You know what I mean, darling. You always know what I mean."

Claire laughed. "Oh, Jos. I've missed you so much."

"You don't have to miss him, Mother? You're here, and we're a family again. Stay, and you won't have to miss either of us ever again."

Claire nodded to Misty, so proud of the woman she'd become. "I've already given up my lease in Lily Dale, dear. I'm home to stay. I'm enjoying my school work tremendously, and have huge plans for next semester."

After supper, Luke spent a few minutes on his laptop Googling, George Washington Claiborne, the third. Old George, as Josiah called him, was a prominent New Orleans businessman. He did, indeed, build number nine Saint Gillian Street for his large family. A landmark in the day. All true.

Did he die in this house? Is that why he's stuck here? That's going to take a lot more investigation.

CHAPTER TWENTY

Thursday, January 19th.

<u>Nine Saint Gillian Street</u>

Luke's grandmother was dressed and sitting at the kitchen table drinking tea with Angelique when he came downstairs. "Gran, you're up. I can't believe how much better you are."

"Lukey, I feel stronger, and I'm so much better, I'd like to go home, today if you have time to take me."

Luke's excitement fell. "Gran, we talked about you staying here permanently. I want you with Misty and me."

His gran set her tea down and gave him a patient smile. "I haven't forgotten, dear, but there are things at my house in the bayou that I want to pack and bring with me. Things I need."

Well, that was a different story altogether. "Okay, why don't we take a trip to Houma, and we'll help you pack up everything you need today."

Misty floated into the room and heard the tail end of

the conversation. "I need a few things from my supplier in Houma. A day trip would be perfect. Can we wait until the girls come?"

Casey came in from the back porch with Hoodoo and poured himself a cup of coffee. Standing shoulder to shoulder, Luke couldn't get over how tall the kid was getting. Tall and slim. He'd shot up so fast he could use a few pounds to fill out a little. "What's for breakfast?"

"Waffles," said Angelique.

"Bless you, Angelique. Have I ever told you how much I love waffles? Almost as much as Farrell."

"Have you seen Walter this morning?" asked Misty.

Angelique pointed to the half-empty dish on the sideboard. "Uh-huh. I think he's done with de basement."

Casey took his coffee to the table and sat down. "I still don't get how he got down there."

Misty shook her head. "The door in the hallway is never open, and he was in a room with the door closed?"

Luke shrugged. "I can't explain it."

"Later, with a new supply of light bulbs, I want to go down there and examine the room he was locked in."

Luke nodded. "Casey and I will help you. I don't want you down there by yourself."

Misty winked at him. "Ah, Lukey, I'm not afraid of George Washington what's his name."

"Might be better if you were, child."

"Why, Daddy? Is he powerful?"

"Not in the way you mean, no. He was never a man of magickal power."

"Why should I be afraid of him then?"

"Because he's a disgruntled old curmudgeon, and others may be helping him rise up against you."

Misty wished her Mother was there to help decipher what her daddy was saying. "What others? I don't know what you mean, Daddy? Is there a ghost conspiracy?"

"Walter has a master, Mystere. Have you not wondered why he was so willing to come here and settle in with y'all."

Misty's mouth dropped open. "You think Walter is a spy for Linc Castille and his brother?"

"A possibility," said Josiah. "Perhaps he'll enlist Old George to help the Castilles.

Casey choked on his coffee. "What? That's crazy."

Misty shrugged. "We'd better get Mother to read Walter's mind again."

Claire walked into the kitchen, smiling. "Why would I want to read that little kitty brain again?"

"Daddy thinks Walter is a spy for Linc and Jefferson."

Her mother burst out laughing and waved away the idea. "Josiah? You are making some wild accusations this morning. Didn't you sleep well?"

"I don't sleep. Remember, my darling."

"I forgot that you're on watch twenty-four seven."

Houma, Louisiana

Luke dropped Misty, Claire, and the students off in Houma to do their shopping while he took his Grandmother home and helped her pack up her belongings. "Put anything you want to take on the kitchen table or on your bed, Gran, and I'll pack it for you. I don't want you lifting anything now that you're doing so much better."

"The healing spell worked wonders on me, Lukey. I don't want to go into the great beyond just yet. Just when things are starting to get interesting."

Luke chuckled. "Living with Misty is interesting, isn't it? She's an amazing person, Gran."

"And you love her."

He nodded. "Yeah. I do."

His gran smiled. "I'm glad, Lukey. You have lots of space in your heart to love. It's good to fill that space with happiness again."

With his grandmother all packed up, Luke drove back to Houma to have lunch with Misty and the kids before they drove home to N'Orlean.

As they enjoyed po' boys in the small diner, a shiver ran through Luke's body.

Misty's gaze narrowed. "What's wrong? You went pale as a sheet, sugar."

Luke stood and tossed a wad of bills on the table. "I have a bad feeling. We need to go home."

Misty nodded. "All right, you heard the man. Grab what you're not finished, and you can eat in the car."

She hurried the kids along and got them all out to the big Ford. Luke helped his Grandmother out of the restaurant and across the parking lot, and he settled her in the front seat. Luke slid behind the wheel, and they were on their way.

Nine Saint Gillian Street

Misty felt it before she saw the dark shroud hanging over the house like clouds hovering low over the mountains. The second and third floors were invisible in the thick fog, the first floor clear and bright. "Do you see it, Luke?"

"I see it."

Luke parked the truck in the lane behind the house, drew his gun, and opened the door of the truck. "Everyone, stay here until I clear the house."

Misty opened the back door of the truck and made a move to get out.

"No, baby. Stay here, please."

He waited until she agreed and then hustled through the back to the door. Using the key, he opened things up and didn't like that Hoo wasn't barking or bouncing down the hall to meet him. "Hoo, where are you?"

The silence was ominous.

"Angelique?" Luke made his way slowly down the hall, ready for an intruder to jump out at him.

Once he reached the kitchen doorway, he saw Angelique, slumped on a kitchen chair. Tied up, her body hung limp like she'd been drugged or knocked out.

Luke ran to her, checked for a pulse, and called 911. He untied her and shifted her to the floor as gently as he could.

He ran back out to continue checking the rest of the house.

"Oh, no." Hoodoo was stretched out in the foyer, and Luke wasn't sure the big dog was breathing. He needed the number for the vet, but first he had to run upstairs and check Misty's room to make sure the book was still there.

Luke dropped to his knees when he saw the damage. Misty's bed was shoved out of the way, the floorboards in her room hacked to smithereens with an ax that was tossed aside, and the hole in the floor was empty. The entire safe was gone.

They stole the Book of Shadows.

Luke ran onto the back porch and waved them forward. "Misty, get the vet info for Hoodoo. Casey, you'll need to take the dog to the vet while Misty and I deal with the situation here."

"What *is* the situation, dear?" asked Claire.

"I've called for an ambulance for Angelique. Charlotte and Michele, go to the front gate and wait for the paramedics, Diana, help Casey with Hoodoo."

Misty dropped to her knees beside her dog, sobbing while Claire tried in vain to revive Angelique.

Sirens screamed down Saint Gillian Street, and the girls waited at the front gate to show the paramedics where Angelique lay unconscious in the kitchen.

That was one trauma taken care of.

"Misty, honey, we need that vet info," Luke said, taking a knee beside her. She was so distraught by Angelique and Hoodoo, she wasn't registering. "*Misty!* Hoo needs help. Where's the vet info?"

Misty got it together enough to find the vet's number on her phone. Luke called and told them Hoodoo would arrive on their doorstep in five minutes. "Okay, baby, you get in the truck. Casey and I will get Hoo."

It took both of them to lift the big lug, but they got him into the truck, and Luke gave Diana Misty's phone with the address. "Go, Casey. Drive Misty, and you two wait with her. I'll handle the police."

The police lights were flashing at the front of the house as Casey drove off. He jogged back inside and met the officers in the front hall. Luke explained what was going on. A robbery with two down.

"What was stolen, sir?"

Luke cursed. With Angelique and Hoo down, he hadn't even thought to tell Misty about the book. "An extremely valuable book. It was kept in a floor safe. The whole safe has been taken." He led the way to the second floor and pointed at the hardwood floor hacked to bits.

"That's one heck of a mess," said the one officer. "Why would they want a book that badly?"

"It was Madam LeJeune's Book of Shadows. It belongs to her family and has been passed down for generations."

One of the officers screwed up his face. "We're talking about a witch book?"

Luke nodded. "Yes, a grimoire, a famous book of spells."

"Any idea who would go to all this trouble to get it?"

"Yes, the same person who has been trying to steal it for the past few weeks—Linc Castille, his brother Jefferson, and possibly their mother, Tilly may have helped him."

The officers made notes and took down Luke's badge number and his credentials. "The crime scene unit will be along shortly, and I'm sure we'll get some dandy prints out of the room and perhaps off the handle of the ax too."

"I'll secure the room, sir. No one will be allowed in there."

While the officers were taking pictures and going about their duty, Luke made tea for his Grandmother. He escorted her into the sitting room at the back of the house and turned on the television. "Relax in here, Gran, until the police are gone. Are you getting any feelings from the intruders?"

"A woman and her two boys."

Luke smiled at his Grandmother. She was older, but still as sharp and perceptive as ever. "Yep. That's what I thought."

University Medical Center

Claire paced in the tiny treatment room as two doctors tried to revive Angelique. They'd taken blood from her arm, and there were no drugs or poisons in her system. It was something else.

It's a spell. But I don't know how to break it.

When the doctors left the room, Claire summoned Josiah.

He was there seconds later, shimmering in the corner of the room. "What can I help you with, darling?"

"The Castilles placed a spell on Madam Angelique, and I need to break the spell before the doctors get back."

"Do you have your wand with you, darling?"

"Always. I always have it with me."

"Repeat after me."

Claire gripped her wand and drew a deep breath to center her power. "Goddess, lend me strength."

> *Spell of harm and unending slumber*
> *I beg the goddess to unencumber*
> *Madam Angelique LaFontaine*
> *Spell be gone, with this wand*
> *Spell I banish, make it vanish*
> *So mote it be*

Claire repeated the spell and directed all the power she could will toward Angelique on the stretcher. Like a light switch flipped, Angelique opened her eyes.

"Where am I?"

Claire exhaled and took her hand. "At the hospital, dear, but we're going home now."

New Orleans Vet Services

Misty could barely stand as the vet assessed Hoo. Her boy took up the whole stainless steel table with his huge body, but as much as she stroked his fur and talked to him, he remained still. He wasn't moving a muscle. She couldn't even tell he was breathing. "Oh, gods, is he dead?"

Casey hugged her. "He's not dead, Misty. He's breathing. I checked."

"Poison would be my first guess," the vet said, gesturing to his assistants to gather what he needed. "We'll do what we can, Miss LeJeune."

Misty couldn't breathe. "You have to save him. Please. Hoodoo has never hurt anybody. People poisoned him. *They* should be the ones here dying."

The vet nodded, looking a little stressed. "Why don't y'all go on home. Hoodoo won't be going home for a couple of days, even if he does survive. As soon as I have something to tell you, I'll call your cell."

Casey gave her a squeeze. "Come on, Misty. Let's go home. We'll come back and see Hoo tomorrow."

"Please be okay, Hoo," sobbed Diana as they departed.

Misty cried all the way to the car, and Diana did too.

Nine Saint Gillian Street

Heartbroken over Hoodoo's precarious health, Misty sobbed as Casey and Diana helped her from the truck to the house. The police were finished their preliminary investigation and were gone. Luke was busy in the kitchen helping Claire make dinner.

"How's Angelique?" asked Misty.

Her mother offered a tired smile. "Better. Resting upstairs until tomorrow. I'll take her a tray when dinner is ready."

"Thank you, Mother. I can barely think straight."

"I should go," said Diana. "The girls have already gone."

"I'll drive you," said Casey. "It's dark, and you shouldn't walk by yourself."

Luke nodded. "Drive her home. Supper will be ready by the time you return." He opened a bottle of wine and poured Misty a glass. "Sit down, baby. Drink a glass of wine."

Misty sat down at the long work table in the kitchen and sipped her wine. "What will I do if Hoo dies?"

"He won't," Casey said, hitting the switch for the porch light and holding the door to show Diana out. "We looked it up. They'll wash out his stomach, and he'll be okay. Maybe even by tomorrow."

"I need to burn healing candles for Hoo." She hopped up off her chair and dragged herself to the step back cupboard. From the bottom section, she pulled out a dozen blue candles and set them in a long row on the table.

Candles wax with smoke and fire
Ignite, I beg you
Flame burn higher

Misty waved her wand in the direction of the candles, and with one loud *poof*, they all ignited at once.

Luke smiled. "Wonderful, sweetheart."

It wasn't enough. She needed to do more. She needed to do everything within her powers to help Hoo heal. "I need a strong healing spell. I'm going upstairs to get the book."

"No," said Luke. "Let's have supper first. Your mother has it all ready and you need something in your stomach."

"I'll just run up and get it before I sit down to eat. Won't take me a minute."

Luke cursed. "No, Misty. I'm sorry, love. The book's not there. The Castilles got it."

Misty stared at Luke, trying to understand what he was telling her. Of course. She'd been so preoccupied with Hoodoo and Angelique she forgot the part about who or why. Fury built inside her like nothing she'd ever felt before. It was hot and angry and exploding from her cells.

Her wand appeared in her hand, and she called a crippling spell down upon the Castilles.

Blood be spilled, and flesh be torn

Bones that ache from night till morn
Hearts that blacken from harm done
Your life you waste till you have none
I curse your lies, I curse your lands
I curse your feet, I curse your hands
I send your evil back to you double
From this day on you know only trouble
Return the book to break the spell
If you don't, you'll burn in hell!

Luke blinked at her as he filled his plate with spaghetti. "That was quite vengeful. Misty, I assure you, I have every intention of getting the book back."

Misty poured herself another glass of wine and became eerily calm. "At midnight, we leave for Houma."

"Excellent decision, child," said Josiah. "Midnight is the perfect hour to set off on a mission of passion."

Claire nodded. "I'll stay with Angelique and Gran."

"Thank you, Mother."

Luke set his plate down and strode to stand in front of her. "I'm not sure retaliation is the way to get the book back."

"How would you suggest?" Misty's question was icy cold.

"Let me think about it."

"You have until half-past eleven."

Luke smiled at her. "My girl has such passion. She's scary as hell at times, but still so beautiful."

CHAPTER TWENTY-ONE

Friday, January 20th.
Midnight.

<u>Broadmoor, New Orleans</u>
Luke started up the truck as Misty and Casey piled in. It was midnight, and he hadn't thought of any better plan than a revenge trip to Houma, so, there you have it. Misty was silent, and Luke regarded her silence as deadly. He'd never seen her at full power although some nights in bed with her, he had fantasized about it. Perhaps some fantasies should be left unfulfilled. This wouldn't be a peaceful night.

"We'll pass by Linc's house here in the city first," Luke said, stopping at the light. "I'll stop and see if anyone is there."

"Make's sense," said Casey. "Why go all that way if the snakes are right here."

Linc's shotgun house sat in full darkness as Luke parked out front. "Casey, you go round the back that way and check windows and doors to see if they're open. I'll

go the other way and meet you in the back. Misty, you—
” He caught the look flashing in her eyes and thought
better of telling her to wait there. “You do whatever you
want, sweetheart. Just don’t make Lukey into a frog,
please. He loves you.”

Luke and Casey set off and, silently as a ghostly
shadow, Misty floated along behind him. There was
nothing at the back of the house, but a broken-down
garage that should have been demolished.

The back porch was missing a couple of boards, and
Luke was careful where he stepped. Wearing a pair of
latex gloves, he tried the door handle. Locked. He pulled
out his lockset and had the door open in half a minute.
“Don’t touch anything unless you’re wearing gloves.”

Casey slipped on an extra pair and followed right
behind Luke. The house was a mess. Dusty, dirty, and all
surfaces piled high with clutter. The man who lived here
was off-center, and cleanliness was not high on his list.

Luke tried the lights. The hall light flicked on
overhead, and that just highlighted more mess. Misty
seemed to be in a trance. “Are you getting any visions of
where the book is, sweetheart?”

“It’s covered and hidden.”

“Make’s sense the Castilles would keep it hidden.”

“The spell is working, but not here.”

“Then, let’s move on,” said Luke.

Houma, Louisiana

Madam Castille’s house was just as dark and lifeless as

Linc's house in the city had been.

Casey huffed. "Where are these people? It took us over an hour to get here, and they're not here."

Luke sighed. "They've run off with the book. We might as well have a look through the house anyway. Might give us a clue to where they've gone."

"What if they've gone into the bayou?" asked Casey.

"Then we'll need a guide to find them." Luke opened the back door of Tilly Castille's house, and seven cats ran out and circled their legs as they tried to step inside.

"Okay, that's spooky. It's like a Hallowe'en house."

They moved from the short back hall into the kitchen.

Casey poked at the goo in the pot on the stove. "Something is cooking, and they didn't turn it off when they left. Smells like frogs."

Luke took a whiff and nodded. "My Grandmother made that potion lots of times when I lived at home."

"What's it for?" asked Casey.

"It's a truth potion."

Casey gave it another poke. "A homemade truth serum? That is way cool. We should bottle some and use it on the ones that made it."

"Sound idea, kid. Let's find some jars."

In his quest for empty jars, Casey kicked one of the empty cat bowls on the floor. He picked it up and read the name on it. "Walter. This is Walter's dish."

They spent hours searching every closet, cupboard, nook, and cranny. The book was not there. The Castilles had taken it with them wherever they had gone.

"Let's go home," said Luke. "We'll deal with this in the morning. The police will have a good chance of tracking them down. Better than us."

As they rounded the house to get to the truck parked at the curb, Misty stood on the sidewalk for a moment with her wand in her hand. She raised both her hands to the moon in the sky and chanted.

> *Wind of the north, I call you forth*
> *Wind of the east, Spin like a beast*
> *Wind of the west, Funnel the rest*
> *Wind of the south, Take this house*
> *So mote it be*

Lightning flashed, and the wind gusted with unrestrained force from all four corners of the sky. A huge spinning funnel descended on Madam Castille house and lifted it off the ground like it weighed nothing. Up and up went the house until it disappeared into the clouds.

Misty jumped into the front of the truck and slammed her door. "Now we go home."

Nine Saint Gillian Street.

Luke sat at the kitchen table drinking coffee the next morning and wondering about how and when the

Castilles had come to steal the book. "Can you remember what happened when the Castilles came, Madam LaFontaine?"

Angelique stopped her cleaning and came to sit opposite him. He was relieved to see her up and almost herself again. "A little. I heard Hoodoo bark one time, d'en he stop. D'at made me think nobody was at de door, so I don't look."

"You didn't hear them come in?" asked Luke. "I set the alarm before we left."

"D'at alarm don't make a sound, Mr. Luke."

"Okay, Linc disabled the alarm remotely before they broke in. What else can you remember?"

"I'm busy makin a batch of de salve for colds and fever. I turn around, and ugly woman points her wand and casts a spell on me. D'at's all I remember."

"The police are looking for the Castilles, and I'm sure Misty will have a few ideas of her own when she gets up."

Luke hated to see Misty suffering. She was sitting at the end of the long work table, wringing a napkin in her hand and saying nothing. Luke had tried talking to her, but she seemed to be in a trance-like state, and she wasn't hearing him.

"Leave her," said Claire. "When she gets like that, you have to wait it out."

"Have you had any insight into where the book might be, Madam?" asked Luke.

"No, but I believe if we put all of our powers together, we might get something. I called the girls to come over after breakfast."

Casey brightened. "The girls are coming?"

"Yes, I've postponed classes until this crisis is averted, but they are anxious to help find the book." Claire trained her gaze on the corner of the kitchen. "Have you come up with any ideas, Josiah, dear?"

"I'm beside myself with worry, darling. The Castilles are a nasty lot, and it horrifies me to think about what they might do with my spells."

"You're right to worry. With that book, the amount of damage that could be done by evil hands is untold."

Casey leaned in and whispered. "Sorry to interrupt. Is it all right if I call the vet to check on Hoo?"

Luke tilted his head towards Misty. "Go ahead, buddy. Do it in the sitting room, would you?"

Casey nodded and went into the room across the hall.

When breakfast was ready, Angelique went upstairs and helped his grandmother down the stairs. Luke gave his Gran a hug and got her set up. "After breakfast, we're going to call the corners. Are you up to going outside for a few minutes, Gran?"

"Oh, my boy. Calling the corners is one of my specialties."

Around nine-thirty, the girls arrived. No barking and Casey hadn't passed on any news, so Luke figured the update on Hoodoo's condition couldn't be good. He'd talk to Casey later in private.

Claire greeted the girls in the foyer and herded them into the kitchen for a chat before they began. Misty sat in her same spot, still staring. Her mother was ignoring her and told everyone else to do the same.

"She'll speak when she's ready. In the meantime, we'll do everything we can to get ready."

"Where's Walter?" asked Charlotte.

"Walter was a spy," said Casey. "He was up to no good. After the Castilles stole the book, Walter was gone."

"The cat was a witch spy?" Charlotte said.

Casey nodded. "A familiar loyal to the enemy."

"Can we get another cat?" asked Diana.

Luke sighed. Life in Misty's house was hectic, even when the world hadn't gone crazy. "Possibly. My Gran likes to have a cat around. I might get her one if Misty's okay with that."

Angelique nodded. "As long as it's not a *grenouille*."

Luke chuckled. "No more frogs."

After breakfast and tea were finished, Claire stood up. She was wearing a long black dress that swirled around her legs when she walked. "Girls, shall we cast the circle and get ready to call the corners?"

"Ooh, yes, please," said Michele.

Claire went out into the yard and began gathering stones to form the circle. "You may have to look in the lane to find as many stones as we will need, girls."

Once they had enough, Claire cleansed the area where she wanted the circle, and then the girls arranged the stones they had gathered. When they were ready, they summoned the others outside into the yard. The wind was brisk, and the January day was chilly, even for New Orleans.

"Now that we're all in the circle and the circle is closed, we'll call the Directions," said Claire.

Misty stood silently beside Luke, watching her mother perform the ritual. He held her icy hand and felt the unleashed power pulsing within her body.

"Guardians of the East, I call you forth to guard my circle. Hail and welcome." Claire repeated the three other directions then she called on the Lord and Lady to help them in their task.

"We need your help to find a lost object." Claire held her hands up high above her head. "A precious book of power was stolen and needs to be found before it is used for ill purpose."

The wind grew bitter as they waited for help to descend from the heavens. The girls shivered as they held hands and maintained the circle.

Diana clutched Casey's hand tighter as the wind swirled sticks, leaves, and dead grass around their legs.

Misty stood and called her lost object home.

Goddess of the Moon and Stars
I beg you restore what's ours
Stolen by evil, one, two, three
Bring my grimoire back to me.
Goddess of the Sun and Moon
Bring my book back to me soon
Punish thieves and evil done
Grant my plea by setting sun
So mote it be.

A jagged fork of lightning flashed across the sky, and the girls screamed as thunder boomed overhead.

Misty levitated, her arms still upraised, and she hovered suspended a foot above the ground in the middle of the circle. Her long dress swirled around her legs. Her long hair blew in a wild tangle around her head.

Claire felt a surge of pride, watching her daughter in all her glory, while everyone stood transfixed.

Once Misty descended and alighted on solid ground, Claire faced the north and began thanking the deities and releasing them. Then she released the quarters and the elements, again thanking them for their participation.

"The circle is open but not broken. Merry meet and merry part. Merry meet again." She bent down and placed both hands on the ground, and everyone followed suit, absorbing the energy still in the circle.

"Well done, all," said Gran. "Now, inside to warm up and restore our spent energies."

Back in the kitchen, the energy was positive once again, and the girls were on a high. "That was the most exciting

258 · AUBURN TEMPEST

thing I've ever done or seen," said Charlotte, her dark eyes wide. "Misty was amazing."

Diana turned to Casey, her cheeks still flushed from the bite of the January wind. "Do you think the Castilles received the message?"

"It was so powerful, how could they not?"

Claire refilled everyone's teacup from a freshly brewed pot. "Oh, we're not finished yet, young witches. Now we'll pool all of our psychic powers and try to get a location."

Misty had lapsed into silent mode again, but she nodded in agreement with her suggestion. "Let's join hands around the table. Concentrate hard, focusing only on the Book of Shadows and try to remember any scrap of information you are given. You all have gifts. All you have to do is train your mind to use them."

With their eyes closed, they all sat perfectly still holding hands for five solid minutes before anyone moved.

Claire let out a breath. "That's long enough for our first try. Everyone write down every detail you can remember, and then we'll go over all the notes."

Angelique set out a tray of vegetables and cheese, and they all started to nibble.

Claire lifted her page and began. "I had a strong vision of a man—possibly Mr. Castille—but he was definitely dead."

"What else, Mother?"

"He stood on the bank of a river."

Luke started his own set of notes and wrote down Claire's impressions. "Gran, did anything come to you?"

"A heavy mist clouded my thoughts and made me think the people we seek are deep in the bayou."

"Okay, that's good. Misty?"

"A fisherman in a pirogue was all I saw. I don't know how that helps us."

"What's a pirogue?" Charlotte asked.

"A little boat," Angelique answered her.

"All signs of the bayou," said Luke. "What else? Casey?"

"I saw the gators sleeping on the banks in the sun. Maybe I was thinking of the bayou and made myself think that, but behind the gators, farther away from the water, I saw a clear image of a shack on stilts."

Angelique nodded. "If d'ey hide in de swamp, we need Marc to guide us."

"Did you see them Madam LaFontaine?"

"Oui. Monsieur Castille perhaps had a fishing shack?"

Luke nodded. "Possible. I can search for it, but most properties in the bayou are unregistered."

Claire pointed at Michele. "Come on girls. Let's hear from the three of y'all."

Michele nodded. "Through the mist, I saw cypress trees and a dock. I didn't see any people."

Diana pushed her short ebony hair away from her face and frowned. "I saw something so weird; I don't know whether to tell y'all or if y'all will laugh at me."

"It doesn't matter how weird it is," said Misty. "It might be a key detail in a different form."

Luke nodded. "Exactly, Diana. Don't hesitate to tell us."

"I saw Walter sitting next to Wannabe, but they weren't at Gran's house where we let Wannabe out."

"Where were they?" asked Casey.

"They were at another place, and I tried to read the name on the sign, but I can't be sure."

"Try," said Casey. "What do you think it said?"

"Rudy?"

Angelique nodded, and Misty got to her feet. "They took a boat from Rudy's Crab Shack."

"Hold on, Mist, we haven't heard from Charlotte yet."

"I don't have much to add," said Charlotte. "All I saw was the book open on a wooden table, and I tried to see what spell it was open to, but I couldn't read it."

"Y'all did amazingly well," said Claire. "It's time to make a plan for tomorrow."

"Tonight, we hold a vigil for Hoo," said Misty. "I'll get   the   candles."

CHAPTER TWENTY-TWO

Saturday, January 21ˢᵗ.

<u>Nine Saint Gillian Street</u>

Luke stood on the back porch, wondering what else could go wrong for the woman he loved. Misty was in such a terrible place with the Book of Shadows missing and Hoo so close to death. He had to do something. People were almost impossible to find in the bayou, and if that's where the Castilles were hiding out with the book, chances of finding them were slim. Angelique had called her youngest son, Marc, and he was coming from Texas to help, but it could be all for nothing.

He trudged back into the house, needing to warm up after standing outside in the brisk January wind. New Orleans was in the midst of an unusual cold snap.

Angelique was busy in the kitchen, getting breakfast started. She'd raised both her boys on the bayou, and they knew the waterways better than most.

"What time do you think Marc will arrive, Madam?"

"He start *tres* early," she said. "*Midi.*"

"We'll be ready to go at noon." Luke poured himself a coffee, and as he passed the large pan of sizzling bacon he realized how hungry he was. Misty had eaten nothing the day before. He'd have to pay attention to that problem today.

Claire rose next, and she brought Gran downstairs with her. "This will be a busy day. Luke, what do you think of the girls going with you to the bayou? I know they asked to go, but too many people will slow you down."

"I've been thinking about it. And you're right. Only Misty, Casey, and I will go with Marc and Angelique. We can't travel through the swamp with ten people."

Misty floated into the kitchen, hearing the tail end of the conversation. "After breakfast, I'm going to the veterinarian's office to spend time with Hoo before we leave."

Luke nodded. "Good idea, sweetheart."

Casey was the last one up, but he was showered, dressed, and ready for the day ahead. "Am I late for breakfast? I could smell bacon."

"*Non* and *oui*," Angelique said. "And I pack a cooler to take in de boat, so you don't go hungry later."

New Orleans Vet Services

Doctor Sanderson escorted Luke, Misty, and Casey to the hospital room at the back of the building where the overnight patients were sleeping. The moment Misty laid eyes on Hoo, she cried. Hoodoo heard her and tried to lift his head. Misty ran across the room and fought to open the door of the cage.

"I'll get that for you, Madam LeJeune. It will do him good to smell you and feel your presence."

"Has he eaten anything?" she asked.

"He drank a little water, and that's a good sign."

"When can I take him home?"

"I'd prefer to watch him for a couple of days more until he's eating and a little stronger. He's a large dog and hasn't eaten nearly enough yet. He sleeps most of the time, and that's good for him. His body needs to recover from his ordeal."

"I'll be out of town for a day or two anyway," said Misty. "Please take good care of him."

"I promise. We take the best possible care of our patients."

Nine Saint Gillian Street

Marc LaFontaine arrived ten minutes after twelve and was greeted by hugs and kisses from his mother. They spoke together so quickly in their Cajun dialect the rest didn't have a clue what they were saying.

After a light lunch, Luke and Marc packed the big Ford with everything they needed to forage deep into bayou country.

"Don't forget bug repellent," said Gran. "You will need it."

"Are you coming, Daddy?" asked Misty. "You went

the last time to Angelique's house. Remember?"

"Of course, I remember, daughter. I'm dead, not senile."

Misty giggled, and it was the first time she'd even smiled since the Castilles stole the book.

Rudy's Crawfish Shack and Boat Rental

Luke drove southwest for an hour and a half, and they reached Rudy's on the edge of the bayou. Luke and Marc stepped inside the small wooden building to rent a boat and to find out if Rudy knew where the Castilles might be. The swamp was a vast labyrinth of channels so confusing, that many a man had been swallowed up and never returned.

As they moved deeper into the crawfish shack, the pungent smell of boiling crawfish overwhelmed. They zig-zagged through the four wooden tables and mismatched chairs to where Rudy stood behind the counter.

There were no customers for the cooked crawfish, and Luke wondered why Rudy bothered with that side of his business. From what Angelique said, Rudy—a small Cajun man in his mid-forties—wore a big smile on his face, even if he was shafting you out of your last nickel.

"Marc, nice to see you, buddy," Rudy held out his hand to Marc. "Long time."

Marc shook Rudy's hand but didn't seem that thrilled about their reunion.

Luke wanted to jump in and say—*Hey, you rented a*

boat to the Castilles. Where are they?—but he knew Bayou folks weren't quick to take to strangers, and didn't like questions.

Marc did the talking, and soon enough, a conversation ensued. Luke wasn't catching much of it until he heard Marc say, "We need de big boat."

"She's ready to go. Forty-dollar deposit, plus extra gas by the can."

Luke opened his wallet, pulled out two twenties, and looked to Marc to estimate how much extra gas they'd need. Marc held up two fingers, and Rudy added on ten bucks more.

At the dock behind the shack, Luke and Casey loaded the stuff from the truck into the boat while Misty and Angelique looked on.

Rudy came outside to supervise and seemed a little too interested in every detail. "Why you want to find the Castilles, Madam LeJeune?"

"It's a private matter, Rudy. Are they paying you to keep watch for them?"

"Lots of folk pay me for lots of reasons."

"The Castilles are dangerous, Rudy," said Misty. She pulled her wand out of her pocket and edged a few steps closer. "Perhaps you need my protection?"

Rudy's dark eyes grew wide, and he nodded his head. "I *do* need protection, Madam. You are de most powerful one."

"Never betray a powerful friend." Misty flicked her wand, and the bare branches on the tree Rudy stood next to burst into flames.

Rudy jumped and bent his knee slightly. "I won't forget, Madam. Rudy never forgets."

<u>LaFontaine Residence, Bayou Country</u>

After an hour of twisting and turning through narrow channels in the swamp, Marc slowed the boat and docked it. They had arrived at the home of Angelique LaFontaine and her two boys, Marc and Luc.

Recently, Luc had spent a couple of months finishing the rebuilding of their home. Where once a one-room shack with no plumbing and no electricity had stood on stilts, now in its place sat a cozy two-bedroom home.

Angelique raised her boys in primitive conditions and had never seen an indoor bathroom or kitchen sink until she moved to New Orleans to become Misty's assistant. Watching her see her newly renovated shack for the first time made her smile.

"Oh, it's so lovely, *mon cher*. Let's go see inside."

Marc had the key to the new door that actually closed, and he led the way. He'd been back here from time to time helping his brother when they had time off from the ranch where they both worked in Texas.

Angelique was in tears as she looked around at all the work the boys had done. Her big black wood stove was still there, but she now had an electric stove, a refrigerator, and a run of cupboards.

"Help me unload the boat, Casey," said Luke. "It'll

be dark soon. We won't search for the Castilles until morning."

Casey nodded and started unloading. "After all the gators we saw on the way here, I wouldn't want to be searching the swamp in the dark."

"Yeah, that's a bad idea." Luke hefted the cooler onto the dock. "Aside from the gators and the snakes that you can't see, nighttime is poacher time. The swamp is full of poachers who come at night and hunt and steal from the traps of the people who live here."

After a simple supper of the warmed-up jambalaya they'd brought with them, Misty and Angelique cleared the table and did the dishes.

"We should ask for guidance for tomorrow," said Misty as she put away the dishes.

"I'll light de candles," said Angelique.

"We are close to the book," said Josiah from the corner of the kitchen.

"I know, Daddy. I feel it too."

CHAPTER TWENTY-THREE

Sunday, January 22nd.

<u>LaFontaine Residence, Bayou Country</u>

Luke woke before dawn, and Misty was gone from the small bed they shared. He rose quietly, tugged on a pair of jeans and picked up his smokes and lighter.

Marc and his mother were talking in the kitchen as Angelique laid the old wooden table for breakfast.

"Morning," said Luke as he passed through the room. The smell of new lumber was evident all through the house. "Seen Misty this morning?"

"She went outside a while ago," said Marc.

Luke stepped out the front door into a thick river mist that made him shiver from the dampness. It seemed to penetrate his skin and chill him to the core, and he realized he should've worn his jacket.

He lit up his first smoke of the morning, vowing to quit as he did almost every morning. Then, he walked around to the back of the house, looking for Misty. At first glance, he didn't see her but then there was a rustling in the woods, and he walked towards the sound. "Misty, where are you?"

"I'm here. Gathering a few things I might need for later."

"Are you planning a new ritual?"

"Nothing specific yet. It doesn't hurt to be prepared."

Luke smiled when he saw her bent down at the foot of a cypress tree, digging in the dirt. "Don't try to snow me. I know when you're doing something magickal. I can hear it in your voice and see it in your green eyes.

"I'm looking for the Lucky Hand root. Can you help me find it?"

Luke glanced around. "Not much sun gets in here, Mist. I don't see any orchids."

"I want to have something ready in case we encounter the three Castilles all at once. We have to stun them, then take the book. I'll leave you to arrest them, or you can do whatever you want with them for robbing our house."

Luke listened to the words Misty was saying, but he wasn't buying into the part where he cuffed the Castilles and hauled them off to jail.

No. That didn't sound like Misty at all. The first thing on her mind would be getting even for Hoo.

"Really, sweetheart? I thought you'd be a little more into payback than that."

Misty shrugged, and Luke knew he was right.

"Before we get the book back or do anything else,

we have to find the Castilles. Let's get an early start."

"Alright. Maybe Angelique knows where the Lucky Hand grows."

Marc backed Rudy's rental boat away from the dock using a pole. The river was too shallow in front of their property to start the motor. That would have to wait until they were in the middle of the channel.

Misty shivered and moved a little closer to Luke. He picked up her hand and held it. "We'll find them. Marc thinks he knows where Mr. Castille used to fish."

"Is he dead, Marc?" asked Misty.

"*Oui*, gator got 'im few years ago."

Casey made a face. He was already on a gator watch.

For the first hour, Marc was able to use the motor, slowing down at some places for logs and debris, then he turned into an offshoot channel that was narrow and shallow. He cut the Merc and stood in the bow of the boat with the pole.

"Slow now," he said. "Gators will be close by."

Casey shifted in his seat and moved to the center of the boat. Luke smiled at him.

Marc stopped poling and pointed to a small wooden shack on the left bank of the narrow channel. "I think dat be the Castilles."

"Okay, great," said Misty. "Thank you, Marc."

He pushed the pole down into the mud six or seven

more times and got the boat as close to the dock as it would go. He hopped out and was looping the rope around one of the posts when a man ran out of the shack and started hollering.

"You can't tie up there. That's our dock."

"Jefferson Castille," whispered Luke. He felt for the gun in his waistband.

Misty jumped onto the dock before Luke could stop her. Instead of coming up against Jefferson, she jumped to the grassy slope and headed up to the shack. He didn't see the wand in her hand at all, but he saw the limb break off the bald cypress that towered above the shack and come crashing down on the roof.

Lincoln and his mother ran outside when the bough crashed, and Misty met them head-on.

Luke was running as fast as he could go with Marc and Casey on his heels.

Linc grabbed Misty, tossed her onto the ground, and grappled with her trying to take her wand.

"Get your hands off her," shouted Luke.

Jefferson blocked his path and took a swing at him, and Luke swung back, whacking Jefferson Castille across the head with the butt of his gun. "Help Misty, Casey."

Luke dropped to the ground to cuff Jefferson's hands.

Casey picked up a big branch and gave Lincoln a hefty whack across the head, and it was enough to knock him away from Misty.

272 · AUBURN TEMPEST

Marc helped her up, and they ran inside the shack looking for the book.

"No, you can't take it back," screamed Madam Castille. She waved her wand in a wide arc, and sparks flew like arrows towards the cabin door.

Casey was on the old woman like sprinkles on a donut. He tackled her around the waist and ran her out of the shack and down into the mud. Luke knew that seeing Hoo lying at the vets, had pissed the kid off, but he was possessed. He wrenched her warped wand out of her hand and chucked it into the river.

"No more," he yelled, fury clear on his face.

She rolled and clawed and screamed curses. Casey wasn't listening. He held that crazy old witch down.

Luke pounced on Lincoln and cuffed him while he was still dazed from the blow Casey had rendered with the branch. Then, he moved on to the mother.

Misty came out onto the porch of the shack, her book clutched to her body with both arms wrapped tightly around it. "I got it, Daddy. We can go home now."

"You will never take the book away from the Castilles." Madam Castille caught Casey across the ear with her elbow and stumbled to her feet to run back toward the cabin.

"The book belongs to the LeJeunes," said Josiah. "You are a thief, Madam, and you will pay for your evil doings."

"You think I'm afraid of a ghost, Josiah? You

always were a pompous old fart. You can do nothing to me."

> *Evil house*
> *Without a spouse*
> *Madam Castille*
> *Become a mouse*

A huge puff of gray smoke filled the air, and where Madam Castille had stood sat a tiny gray mouse. Josiah wasn't finished.

> *You have no fear, No shiver or shake*
> *I cast your lot as lunch for a snake*

Out of nowhere, a long black snake slithered into the mix. His tongue darted out, and the mouse was gone.

"That was amazing, Daddy. You've still got it."

Luke, Marc, and Casey herded the Castille brothers to the boat and sat one in the bow and the other in the stern so they could keep watchful eyes on them.

Misty sat in the middle seat with Casey. She was still clutching the LeJeune Book of Shadows tightly to her body.

"We did it, Misty," said Casey. "We got the book back."

"We did. Now, the only thing we need is to get Hoodoo home, safe and healthy."

"We'll go see him as soon as we get back," said Luke. "I bet he'll be sitting up and barking to get home."

Marc propelled them out of the narrow channel using the pole, and when they were safely in deeper water, he started the motor for the trip back to LaFontaine's.

For the first forty-five minutes of the journey, the Castille brothers were silent, and they sat perfectly still with their hands cuffed behind their backs.

Luke silently congratulated himself for a job well done. When they got back to N'Orlean, he would call the police and have them picked up and charged for their crimes. Too bad about their mother. Lincoln and Jefferson hadn't seen the snake gobble her up, and that was probably for the best.

"We're almost there," said Marc as the channel narrowed. They passed another shack and floated along, a few feet from a dock with a pirogue tied there bobbing.

Lincoln saw the boat and launched to his feet. Before anyone could stop him, he plunged into the water, splashing wildly, trying to get to the dock.

The splashing attracted attention from the inhabitants on the opposite bank, and three immense gators slithered into the water without making a sound. They disappeared under the black swamp water, and then with one loud snap, Lincoln was pulled under.

He disappeared, and that triggered a scream from his brother Jefferson, who toppled over the side in a futile effort to save his brother.

"I should have brought zip-ties for their ankles," said Luke when the blood floated to the top of the water.

Casey nodded. "Yep. That would have been good."

EPILOGUE

Monday, January 23rd.

<u>Nine Saint Gillian Street</u>

Charlotte, Michele, and Diana showed up for school and were thrilled to discover that the LeJeune Book of Shadows had been recovered. "I wish we could have gone with y'all," said Diana. "I want to hear all about it."

Casey nodded, wondering what parts he should leave out. Maybe all of it. "It was an adventure."

"And now that we have the book back," said Claire, "we can get back to our classes. Everybody upstairs, we have tons of work to do."

"I'll be along in a little while," said Misty. "First, we have to go pick up Hoo. He's well enough to come home today."

The girls all cheered, and Luke handed Misty her coat. "You ready, sweetheart."

Misty smiled at the chaos of her home and couldn't believe all the changes in the past month. The best part, she wasn't alone anymore. There was enough love and magick in nine Saint Gillian to keep them all busy for a very long time.

Or, at least until the next crisis hit.

~ THE END ~

Thank you for reading, and since you're here, for still reading.

Mom and I hope you enjoyed our first collaborative storytelling. Mystere LeJeune is one of her (Carolina Mac) characters from her Blackmore Agency series, and when she fell in love with a trilogy cover set that our very talented friend, Heather Hamilton-Senter created (Book Cover Artistry) she wanted to see how Misty would do with an urban fantasy spinoff.

Fantasy, magic, and make-believe are more in my wheelhouse, so we decided to try it together. Normally, I write steamy fantasy romance (JL Madore), so this was different for me too. I think the result is a blended mix of both our styles.

Series reading order:

School for Reluctant Witches
School for Saucy Sorceresses
School for Unwitting Wiccans
Nine Saint Gillian Street
The Ghost of Pirate Alley
Jinxing Jackson Square

And please, if you enjoyed the story, give it a rating and/or a review on Amazon. It not only helps us as the authors, but also other readers find something new to read.

As always, we love to hear from our readers. You can find us both on Facebook.

Blessed Be

CPSIA information can be obtained
at www.ICGtesting.com
Printed in the USA
LVHW112142221122
733851LV00022B/576